The legend of
'red jade talisman'

by Tseng Hsiang-Yun

Printed in Taiwan, Republic of China

For information address:

Elephant White Cultural Enterprise Ltd. Press,

8F.-2, No.1, Keji Rd., Dali Dist., Taichung City 41264, Taiwan (R.O.C.)

Distributed by Elephant White Cultural Enterprise Co., Ltd.

ISBN: 978-986-5526-45-0

Suggested Price: **NT$200**

Foreword

The accident of rooftop

In the mid night, every thing is silent.

There are only a few sounds of cars and people from street occasionally.

Gu chang zch is climbing the stairs step by step, 'pa''pa''pa', goes to the rooftop of tenth floor in Xiangyun building.

He climbs the stairs instead of taking elevator, just hopes the next thing that he will want to do becoming more serious.

As he has finished the last step, he just stands on the rooftop, sees the scene under foot from the highest point of this building.

The weak neon lighting between the builds which look like sword bombs, twinkles still.

Gu chang zch feels confused: he is a so bad—luck man.

A week ago, his girl friend Ju e officially broke up with him.

Ju e stammered：Although she hoped that she can stay with him forever, but, she discovered they were not perfect couple finally, thanked his love, however, he and she would also be the good friends late.

Gu chang zch listened to her lines，quite understood: she finished their love because she found out another rich young man to be her new lover.

In the meaning time, he was fired on the architect company for economic depression.

As he just looked for the new job on the net, his cousin came in and told him:

'I need to sell the house, then, immigrate to aboard, so, I am so sorry that you can not live here any longer. '

'It is nothing, woman, job, residence, you can get new all of them, right? '

Every body would say that.

Gu chang zch just indulges in deep sorrow.

Now, he only wants to jump from here——makes his all pains disappear.

His body is right next to the edge of rooftop.

Suddenly, a flesh of light with seven colors is passing the urban landscape in front of him, then, it has stopped whole half hours and vanishes.

'What was it? '

'Dose rainbow of night fall down the land because of astronomical change?'

'Who cares? '

'Even though the earth breaks down, it is not my own business too. '

His body leaned down more.

A hand touches his shoulder unexpectedly.

He turns head, sees an old man with matted white hair, long eye brows, and sparkling eyes— looks like a quite powerful person.
'Although you are an old man, you still do not have the right to disturb anybody' s suicide. '
Gu chang zch said angrily.
'You would not die absolutely. '
'God of "red jade talisman" already chose you. '
The old man had firmly manner.
'God of "red jade talisman"?'
'What kind of thing is this? '
'It is just funny to meet a nonsense old man before I die. '
Gu chang zch muttered in his heart.
'The life became so worse, then, you lost all interesting to it once in a while. '
'Just thought finishing the life as soon as possible.'
'I had been in this stage too. '
The old man relieved.
'Would you like come to my home, spend a little time gossiping with me? '
He inquired about Gu chang zch.
'It is unnecessary. '
Gu chang zch blurted out.

But, his body is set for the old man's light in his eyes.

The light looks like from deep cave, launches into man's soul,

enforces him to explore some thing.

He just hangs here, can not move.

Contents

Part one

Seven elites in Tao faction

Only a little time, Gu chang zch already has got into a stone world from the dead roof top .

There are different kinds of stones in a narrow living room.

Various colors and shapes: water red, light green, shallow yellow, usual black and brown...

lunar, rectangle, circle, lotus, lion head, even flute, knife...

It is too unbelievable!

'All stones are natural, not artificial, right? '

Gu chang zch has not yet recovered from his surprise in this stone world—a scent flutters over.

The old man asks him come to table to eat something.

'Wow! '

Gu chang zch marvels at the dishes in front of him.

All appliances are made by stones.

Stone roast meat, pickle is put on the small light blue stone bowl, oat cakes are arranged with a stone plate, turnip soup is taking heat in the stone soup pot .

The wine which is filled in a pair of stone goblets gives a seductive color.

'Even I die, also want to be stuff. '

Gu chang zch talked by himself.

He sits down and enjoys all dishes on the dinning table.

The old man relaxes for his good appetizer by the side.

'After finishing this meal, I maybe come back the rooftop again. '

Gu chang zch is still in the dull.

The old man just smiles ; he seemed to have something telling Gu chang zch.

'Most of stones were collected by my father. '

He said, then, drinks one bite of wine.

'He was a Chinese medicine doctor. '

'He was favor on these stones— thought them to be sturdy and have spirituality from nature. '

'So, when I was a child, had already seen so many strange stones, and I am also used to the weird for them. '

He scratched his sideburns a little.

'Once, he brought a blood red, shine jade that was similar to talisman, wrapped with the white silk which had red patterns. '

'He did not put the red jade with other stones unusually, just hided it privately. '

'My father even did not say an word to this special stone, but, his expression was such complex...'

'Surprised, shocked, some worried and disturbed. '

The old man became a little heavy, as to have a bite of wine again.

'Since, after he had diagnoses patients, he just took the little thing to rube their meridians, once in a while, they could relieve the pains and have good spirits. '

'Dose it have another medical effect? '

Gu chang zch plugged and asked.

'Yes! '

'My father himself was also a beneficiary. '

'The jade seemed to make his body be stronger than before, muscle contracted, white hair became less. '

'The whole person looked losing ten years at least. '

Gu chang zch shakes his head and his face takes an incredible look.

'However, the world is hard to predict, '

The old man sighed.

'One day, I came back home after I had been off duty from the bank usually. '

'found the door to be opened, then, I got into the room...'

'Just saw my father falling down in the blood,a small knife inserted the center position of his heart, almost died! '

'I helped him up,afterwards, he opened his eyes, smiled at me ﹐was reluctantly to say:

"There is still time, "

"Move the closet in my bed room, you will see a dark cabinet on the wall. "

"Open it, the things are in it can explain everything. "

after that, he just closed eyes.

  'Icould not help hysterical yelling! '

The old man clenched his fist, was full back to the misery of that year.

Gu chang zch just looked a bit nervous.

'Since childhood, my mother had already passed away, after I grow up, father also died abruptly. '

'I nearly collapsed, would not live normally in a period of time. '

'Through a month, the dark cabinet was just opened. '

He moaned.

'Inside, there were a few items : mahogany sword, Taoist magic paper, incense burner, holy grail, plate, which are used practicing of Taoism. '

'A book...'

He improved the sound.

'Its name is"The profoundness of heaven"——a collection which Tao faction regards it as a standard. '

'Its pages were sandwiched a letter. '

'My father mentioned his past in this letter. '

'He had been a baby who was abandoned on roadside. '

'Fortunately, a Taoist ——Wu Tia nji picked up him and adopted him. '

'Besides, he named my father Wu Hao ying .'

'Wu Tia nji also recruited six children as disciples, plused my father, called them" Seven elites in Tao faction"! '

 'He taught them about skills of Tao faction, charms, self defense, and principles of medical science. '

'Several children got together, quarreled and fraught inevitably. '

'At that time, they were pure and innocent yet. '

'Until adults, but became…'

He thought for a while, then, continued:

'Apparently, " Seven elites in Tao faction" knew how to be modest and polite, '

'They just compared with each other and filled with intrigue secretly. '

'"Standard life"!'

Gu chang zch throw such a sentence rudely.

'Wu Tia nji had a precious thing—"red jade talisman". '

'It is both a jade and a talisman— you can take it to cast a spell on people and to break curses. '

'Furthermore, this jade talisman also has the effects of building up people's bodies as well as flatting their hearts. '

'Most important, it is a" symbol"! '

The old man reached out his index finger, emphasized.

'If you own it, you will have supreme authority in Tao faction. '

'Many people are covetous of it. '

'In" Seven elites in Tao faction", father and his co disciple —Li Yan, had highest talents and best performances about Tao learning. '

'Of course, they had larger opportunity to inherit the"red jade talisman"than other persons. '

Talking about it, the old man covered one layer of worry on his face.

'Li Yan even was more active and bold, had a higher level of accomplishment in Tao faction. '

'However, Wu Tia nji considered his power was too strong,he himself was too ruthless to go to right path. '

'Wu Tia nji settled on my father who was kindly and amiable to succeed to"red jade talisman"more. '

'After all, a top Taoist whose ability and morality must be in the balance.'

Gu chang zch approved of it with a slight nod of his head.

'Unexpectedly, '

The old man raised his voice again unconsciously.

'His disciples discovered that Wu Tia nji just never mentioned the"red jade talisman"in his will, after he had passed on. '

'They also could not find out it on his relics. '

'It should be that master did not want to raise the fight among disciples'.

Gu chang zch gazed at grains of stoneware, said lowly.

'But some mysteries underlay the affair...'

The old man wore a deep and unpredictable look.

' On Wu Tia nji's bedroom, a portrait was hanged on the wall. '

'It was the forebear of Tao faction　—Heaven Leader! '

'He wore yellow robe, carried the dragon sword, clothes were floating, and his ling were pine tree and cloud. '

'My father was very fond of the portrait, often went to see it. '

'Wu Tia nji promised him: "Once I leaves the world, the portrait will belong to you. "'

"When my father took down the portrait from the wall, just kept the eyes out the drawing axis to have slit, it seemed that it could be turned on..."

'Really, it was hollow,a white pebble was put inside. '

'A few small words were engraved on its top...'

'Thousands of mountains, strange stones are lofty and steep, the storm clouds raise in clean field, "jade talisman" is apparent'. '

The old man mourned.

'Line between words, suggested the existence of "red jade talisman". '

' However, you could not full understand it. '

He shock his head in confusion.

'My father kept the white pebble. '

'Also enjoyed gathering the stones for the words" strange stones are lofty and steep" on it. '

'" Seven elites in Tao faction "lost their leader——Wu Tia nji, and forasmuch some participants of it begun to be in league with the corrupt officials by their skills of Tao faction. '

'Father declined to go along with them in their evil deeds. '

'He gave up the skills of Tao faction, practiced medicine, became a Chinese medicine doctor. '

'Late, he married my mother, but, she died earlier. '

'My father had to been wearing two hats as father and mother. '

'The life was so hard to him! '

The old man could say nothing but sigh.

'After more than twenty years, '

'He gradually forgot all thing about "red jade talisman". '

'One time, he lost the way in wildness for his stone collection. '

'Just saw a quaint, Japanese style bungalow by chance! '

His face lines are tight, seemed to come to the main point of depiction.

'On the door of it, there are some words: " Storm clouds house. ". '

'One shout of his brain, he made out the words" storm clouds" on the white pebble to refer to" storm clouds house. ".'

'The surrounding of the bungalow also met the means of "thousands of mountains, strange stones are lofty and steep". '

'He knocked the door of it immediately. '

'The person who answered the door was...'

'Wu Tia nji, unexpectedly!'

'Yean! '

Gu chang zch screamed gently.

'Subsequently, it was clear to my father...'

'The person was twin brother of Wu Tia nji—Wu Tia zhi! '

'Since Wu Tia nji got into Tao faction, rarely dealt with relatives and friends. '

'He just handed "red jade talisman"to Wu Tia zhi at the end of life. '

'Believed that the people whom he chose would take the priceless treasure from his twin brother!'

The old man said sincerely.

Gu chang zch was so moved ；Wu Tia nji—a great Taoist, just used the method with many twists and turns to protect 'red jade talisman' and disciples.

'My father told Wu Tia zhi about the words which he had found on white pebble. '

'He invited him to enter the house...'

'Narrated the story that Wu Tia nji asked him collect "red jade talisman" secretly, next, he just offered my father the supreme thing of Tao faction! '

'It was safer that my father hided "red jade talisman"privately. '

'He just did not think so. '

'He took the precious thing to help patients. '

The old man showed a look of praise to his father.

'Finally, it caused him to die and "red jade talisman" to be stolen. '

'At the end of letter, my father expressed:

If I could read this letter, he might die, in addition, "red jade talisman" was surely taken away.

He gave me another indication that I had to look for"red jade talisman", then, handed it over to the virtue, made sure it was used correctly. '

"In the process of searching, "

'I consumed a lot of money, mental, strength...'

'Had been deceived.'

'Offended friends and relatives, even sacrificed love, marriage. '

'Simultaneously, I expected to catch the murder. '

The old man said word by word, highlighted his will.

'That is it, decades passed…'

'I becomes an old guy! '

He wearied head down.

Gu chang zch looks him sadly.

'Furthermore, my father pointed out of the letter:

"The"red jade talisman"issues the light like a rainbow in every ten years. "

'I had lived on Xiangyun building. '

' Ten years ago, the same late night, I eve saw the light that was
   same as we just met on rooftop. '

'I am convinced that it was the light of"red jade talisman"! '

"The second day, I tried to search the trace of"red jade talisman"in this place where was miles around

that" redjadetalisman"glowed! "

'But nothing.'

The old man showed a little tired involuntarily.

'After ten years, the same moment, I came back the rooftop of Xiangyun building, '

'Wished I could see the light again. '

'Coincidentally, I met you! '

'May I have your name? '

He asked Gu chang zch whom was playing with chopsticks.

'Gu chang zch.'

'Good! Gu chang zch, chang zch! '

'I am Wu Maolin. '

The old man introduced himself.

'You can call me uncle lin. '

'An old man who is mindless and his limbs are inflexible. '

'I had told you God of 'red jade talisman' already chose you. ". '

"So, you must replace me to look for "red jade talisman"! "

He worded with expectation.

'Oh, no!'

Gu chang zch shouted.

'A meal 's price is rather expensive! '

He almost jumped up.

'I hire you! '

Wu Maolin was watching Gu chang zch steadily.

'We newly developed the"pizza bread", please ask the old customer to taste. '

Gu chang zch is so happy and moved to get the hot, fluffy bread which is placed in a paper bag from Jiang Yihui.

He often visits the'Jubilance' bakery, does not particularly fond of its breads, but clings to its human taste.

The boss of"Jubilance"bakery——Jiang Yihui, a kind smile that never changes, a cordial service, makes anyone who sees her feel ease.

Although Gu chang zch thinks that she has a bit over——

enthusiastic.

'How did I not see you for a while? '

Jiang Yihui asked Gu chang zch.

'I had some trouble. '

His words reserved.

Jiang Yihui did not ask more questions.

She knows Gu chang zch a lot, they had talked each other before.

Since his parents divorced, he just became a wanderer—took turns to live with various relatives.

After entering working place, he also had many bumps.

'I have changed work. '

'Help people investigate things. '

Gu chang zch straightened his spine, showed hope and enthusiasm for work.

'You switched to Sherlock Holmes. '

Jiang Yihui teased him.

A burst of firecrackers and a drum sound are coming from outside.

Their eyes fall out of the window coincidentally.

Originally, there is a candidate to canvass on the street.

Gu chang zch looks a little in a hurry.

He checks out for the green union bread, then, he pushes the door away hastily.

'Welcome to come often! '

Against his back, Jiang Yihui said as usual.

On her business smile, also showed a touch of warmth and

compassion.

Li Yuanhu, the hot legislator candidate this time.

He covers with red ribbon, surrounded by a group of people.

With the dragon and lion dance, Li Yuanhu is great in strength and impetus to fight for votes.

Gu chang zch is watching him not far away.

Further described according to Wu Maolin:

Li Yan made some people to get promoted and get rich by his skills of Tao faction.

He himself also became a dignitary.

On the one hand: showing off, on the one hand: reminding.

Li Yan tattooed a black puppy flower on his arm, thought a person who was spicy and domineering in the same way as black puppy flower could board the peak of life.

He also asked future generations to do this.

Gu chang zch guesses that Li Yan was number one suspect who stole 'red jade talisman 'and killed Wu Hao ying.

Even though he died, his descendants should be involved in this matter.

Gu chang zch comes to the street this moment not for some green union bread, just wants to explore Li Yuanhu's reality.

Today, the temperature is high!

Li Yuanhu wears a clean white shirt with short sleeves.

A fan rushes forward to pull his sleeve.

'"Red jade talisman"!'

Gu chang zch bellowed.

He just saw a small red jade which is set in the center of black puppy flower on Li Yuanhu's left arm.

Immediately, Gu chang zch rushes forward, wants to take a close look to his target person.

Accidentally, he loses balance, has a fall, the paper bags drops down — a few pieces of bread are rolling out.

One person raises him.

Gu chang zch looks up...

A young man, puts on jeans and T shirt, looks so healthy and smart.

Just stares at him like a trial.

'A little red dot of black puppy flower is not"red jade talisman". '

The young man explained.

Gu chang zch is slow regaining his consciousness, tries to stand up...

The young man is just busy pulling his hand, forced says:

'Follow me. '

'You can see the panorama of the Danshui river from this window. '

The young man said, aimed at the window.

He just took Gu chang zch to his home by a taxI .

'That is just this...'

'If it was not because of beauty, no one would live in this narrow and stuffy loft. '

Gu chang zch thought.

The young man gets out the medicine box to heal the bruise when Gu chang zch fell, disinfects, puts on liquid medicine.

' OK, it is just a little hurt. '

He applied the tape to the wound finally, said easily.

Gu chang zch says 'thank you' to him.

'You shouted at "red jade talisman" to the little red dot of black puppy flower on the street just now. '

'I know you are the comrade who seeks "red jade talisman".

Young man closed up the medicine box and wiped his hands.

'Wu Tia nji passed the "red jade talisman" to his disciple——Wu Hao ying. '

'Soon, after Wu Hao ying was killed and "red jade talisman" was missing too. '

'The news got out, caused many Taoist to chase this thing. '

'Other six people of " Seven elites in Tao faction" were more passionate about it! '

Mentioned this, young man's eye brows shrinked, it seemed that he trapped some doubt.

'Some people said that one of six people struck a pose...'

'He himself was just the person who killed Wu Hao ying and took over "red jade talisman". '

'He hinted that the person was Li Yan? '

Gu chang zch secretly guessed.

'After all, "red jade talisman's whereabouts had been utterly unknown in their generation. '

'After they died ,the task of finding thing was passed on to their children, even to grandsons, great grandsons...'

'Be sure to reproduce the rare treasure to the world! '

'Are you descendant of the six? '

Young man asked Gu chang zch.

'No, I was just employed for Wu Hao yings'son——Wu Maolin to look for"red jade talisman". '

Gu chang zch answered sheepishly.

'And you? '

He asked the young man.

'Drink beer? '

'Yes, please. '

Young man opens refrigerator, takes out two cans of green island beer, tosses one can to Gu chang zch, then, he turns on another one.

After drinking most of the can, the young man just thoughtfully says :

'Most people firmly believed that Wu Hao ying and Li Yan were the best in" Seven elites in Tao fraction', called them "double jades". '

'But, there was another one ——Yang Jingsong. '

'His Tao skill was not under them. '

'He was just a hermit. '

'Was used to keep himself in the room ——painted, practiced words, played instruments...'

Young man smiled.

Gu chang zch is not sure if the young man appreciates Yang Jingsong.

'And he was still very concerned about people and thing around him. '

'He was relived that Wu Hao ying kept"red jade talisman". '

'After all, '

'Wu Hao ying had both talent and virtue. '

'However, the thing had changed...'

'So he joined the rank of looking for"red jade talisman". '

'Wanted to find it after, handed over to the right person .'

'Yang Jingsong was consistent with Wu Hao ying s'wish. '

Gu chang zch appreciated it at the bottom of his heart.

'This mission passed to his forth generation...'

'I am just Yang Jingsong's great grandson—Yang Ru! '

'We can cooperate to find"red jade talisman". '

'Do more with less. '

Yang Ru confidently stared at Gu chang zch.

Facing the young man whom he just met, Gu chang zch hesitates.

'Yang Jingsong's great grandson—Yang Ru, it is a bit of relationship with me. '

Wu Maolin said, he just tasted sweet potatoes soup with Gu chang zch.

After returning to Wu Maolin's residence, Gu chang zch could not wait to talk about Yang Ru' s variety for the old man.

'The young fellow is about 27 or 28 years old, isn't he ?'

Wu Maolin had a small piece of sweet potato, supposed.

'The new generation must have many new ideas and creativity. '

'He should be able to break through the dilemma that " Seven elites in Tao faction"for generations had not yet found out"red jade talisman". '

He gives Gu chang zch an indication with his eyes.

Gu chang zch, Yang Ru stand the rooftop in Xiangyun building.

An active urban landscape is under their foot.

'You, uncle lin had seen the light of "red jade talisman"on this area. '

Yang Ru made a gesture on the right hand side.

'We should still search the same place. '

He speculated.

'Uncle lin did not have any harvest there. '

Gu chang zch recalled Wu Maolin's fatigue.

'How much do you know about"red jade talisman"?

Yang Ru turned his face to Gu chang zch.

'It has medical effect, also can be used as a spell. '

'It is aura, shines every ten years. '

Gu chang zch answered.

'Not only that...'

Yang Ru smiled in disapproval.

'My great grandfather wrote the things about"red jade talisman"
and" Seven elites in Tao faction"for generations could become a
thick book. '

'The"red jade talisman"also can be manipulated to confuse people
and kill people without spilling blood. '

'Its power is so hard to imagine! '

'Therefore, the object must be improperly for bad guy. '

Yang Ru spoke sincerely and earnestly.

'Modern metropolis: code of science and civilization! '

He focused on the view of the city after a minute or two, then, said.

'People also more believe science ; think it is logic, accurate, has a
basis. '

'I am just concerned with the spiritual energy of the person! '

'Taoism is the absolute concentration of human spiritual will and
the ultimate exertion of human potential. '

He spoke forcefully.

'Except Wu Hao ying, Li Yan, Yang Jingsong, What do you know
about the remaining four of" Seven elites in Tao faction"? '

Yang Rui asked Gu chang zch.

'Listen to you. '

'The principle of Taoism is" passing a man is not a woman". '

Yang Ru said slowly.

'But there was a woman of" Seven elites in Tao faction". '

'Her name was Ning Yuhua. '

'She was the maid's daughter in Wu Tia nji's home. '

'Wu Tia nji saw her being intelligent and have lightweight bone. '

'Recruited her as a disciple.'

'Broke with tradition of Tao faction !'

'But woman has limitations in congenital physiology and physical fitness. '

'Ning Yuhua did not go deep into the Tao. '

'She married early to go abroad, got out of the circle. '

He shrugged helplessly.

'Speaking of foreign country, '

'Have you heard of Japanese ninjutsu? '

'Chinese Taoism has similarities with Japanese ninjutsu. '

Yang Ru asked a question and answered it himself.

'One of" Seven elites in Tao faction"was a Japanese, called Yuan Zhi Jian. '

'He was born a ninja family. '

'Was brought to Taiwan since childhood, joined the Taoist group. '

'Hoped that he would be able to integrate Tao into the ninjutsu and could make ninjutsu to further develop in the future!'

'Yuan Zhi Jian also looked for"red jade talisman"for a while. '

'Afterwards, he gave up, went back Japan. '

'In this Taoist elite organization.'

'Not every one was excellent person...'

'There was a name called He Lei. '

'Had neither learning nor skill.'

'He was funny, like a clown. '

'Everyone regarded him as"a barrel of laughter". '

'Did not care about his other thing.'

'The last one to talk about...'

It seemed to be a bit confusing to Yang Ru, said that the person is about to mention is quite complicated.

'Once shaved as a monk, his Dhama name was Hui Quan. '

'He skillfully used the identity of the monk, created a transcendent image. '

'frequently contacted with wealthy businessman and political celebrities. '

'He cleverly used Taoism in human relationships. '

'Gained both fame and wealth thus.'

'Master Hui Quan, his original name was Yan changrong. '

'Was actually an ordinary monk!'

He said with a very emphatic pronunciation' ordinary monk'.

'Human world!'

Gu chang zch remarked ironically.

'Hui Quan had another stunt, '

'That was proficient in making all kinds of delicate crafts. '

'One of most powerful one was "Seven layers of peals tower". '

'According my great grand father's description, '

'It was made up of hundreds of pearls. '

'My great grand father also had painted the"Seven layers of pearls tower". '

'It was not a a general pagoda type. '

'But liked a tornado!"

There is a surprised express on Gu chang zch's face, Yang Ru just smiles indifferently.

'"Seven layers of pearls tower"was not just a ornament. '

'But a hidden weapon!'

'It could put people to death! '

His shoulder twitched inadvertently.

'"Seven layers of pearls tower"could launch a flying knife on each layer. '

'Each layer of emission method was different. '

'Hui Quan just never mentioned these different methods to people. '

Yang Ru' s tone was a bit heavy.

'I heard that uncle Lin said...'

'When his father——Wu Hao ying died, a knife was inserted in his chest. '

'Would it be? ...'

Gu chang zch doubted.

'It was already unknown. '

Yang Ru gently said.

'Hui Quan once married someone, before he was a monk. '

'Had a son——Yan Wenqi.'

'Yan Wenqi should have inherited the"Seven layers of peals tower". '

He went on speaking.

'Lucky to see you!'

Yang Ru suddenly grinned at Gu chang zch.

' How could you say that? '

Gu chang zch laughed in spite of himself, he always thought he should be a jink.

'Let me know the area where the"red jade talisman"was shinning. '

'Plus the"Seven layers of peals tower"just mentioned. '

'This gives me some sort of assumptions. '

He kept people guessing.

'One year ago, '

'I used to be a newspaper reporter. '

'Ran around the street to interview the news.'

'It is quite familiar with Taipei. '

'The area where light appeared is largest distribution center for computers and electrical appliances——' "Doming Street"! '

Yang Ru was sure to judge.

'1 o'clock, tomorrow afternoon...'

'We meet the street junction of"Doming Street"! '

Yang Ru made such an appointment with Gu chang zch unexpectedly 。

1: 30, the next afternoon.

Gu chang zch is waiting at the street junction of"Doming Street".

A graceful girl comes over face to face.

'What kind of play is it? '

Gu chang zch is too surprised；Yang Ru actually pretend to be a woman, golden long curly hair, orange dress, yellow silk scarf around the'neck'.

He is also very good at dressing up: carefully portrayed facial features, the figure is exquisitely decorated.

What is rare is that he can show the paces and manners of woman.

'Looking for"red jade talisman"is risky. '

'Changed appearance, can cover people's eyes and ears. '

Yang Ru's voice was also transformed into be sweet and feminine.

'We can make a couple! '

He smiles mischievously, holds Gu chang zch to street center.

They stopped at called'Hui qui 'appliance shop.

'How do you think about such an item? '

Yang Ru pointed to a flashlight in the window, asked.

'Decoration is too strong! '

'Its outer shell in addition to curving ,is also decorated with many small bulbs. '

'The shape is distorted, would not be easy to use. '

'And it is too over price! '

Against the '3500' price tag, Gu chang zch pouted.

'You have a quite a lot of ideas! '

Yang Ru gave Gu chang zch a slighted wicked grin.

'I only have one idea! '

'It was based on "Seven layers of pearls tower" and created! '

'I had inquired about it…'

'The owner of the appliance shop is called Yan Chenzhao. '

'About forty or fifty years, '

'He must be the grandson of Hui Quan, that is Yan changrong. '

'He inherited the "Seven layers of pearls tower" to create the shape of this appliance. '

Yang Rui throw a quick glance at the flash light.

'You mentioned it too…'

He looked at Gu chang zch, recalled.

'Wu Hao ying died, a knife was inserted in his chest. '

' That was very likely…'

'Hui Quan fired a short knife from "Seven layers of peals tower' to kill him. '

'Won the "red jade talisman".'

'Later, it was passed to the hands of his grand son—Yan Chenzhao. '

'He hid it in the shop. '

'Accordingly, you could see the light of "red jade talisman" appearing around here. '

He made a gesture of sweeping to the right.

'Have we found"red jade talisman"? '

Gu chang zch asked in a trembling voice.

'The matter is settling into shape…'

Yang Ru said calmly.

'Unfortunately, '

'This is public holiday of this shop──Monday. '

Yang Ru looked at the deep lock shop door.

'It's bound to come again! '

When they come back to this' Hui qui 'appliance shop ，

The situation has changed!

The whole shop was surrounded.

A group of police are entering and leaving.

'What's the matter, Officer Zheng? '

Yang Ru grabbed a tall man, asked.

Gu chang zch unexpected:

'The bizarre young man also has a acquaintance in police community. '

'The owner here was killed! '

'According to preliminary estimated, '

'The murder should enter from the window…'

'The deceased was killed about three or four o'clock in the middle of night. '

'The owner of mobile phone shop next door discovered this store had not opened the door...'

'Felt that some thing was wrong, '

'Looked for somebody to open door, '

'Found the corpse, then, called police. '

'Now, we had already completed the test. '

'The corpse was sent to Forensic doctor Department. '

'We will also investigate the case right away. '

Officer Zheng was relived a little.

Yang Ru stands and thinks about it.

He pulls Officer Zheng aside, whispers:

'May I come in to see it? '

'You know...'

Officer Zheng said in a dilemma.

'I should not make you feel bad. '

Yang Ru nodded meekly first.

Immediately, his eyes turns from gentleness to sharpness.

'Officer Zheng, '

'I even wrote an editorial to argue for you. '

'Ran around, found clues to solve the cases for you.'

'You owes me a favor. '

His tone was very strong.

'Someone had been killed, '

'The murder is like to relate to the treasure I inquire about. '

'If you can let me view the murder scene,'

'Maybe I can find something, '

'Reduce some unnecessary sacrifices. '

Saw Officer Zheng still hesitating, Yang Ru continued to lobby him.

'No touch, just observe. '

'fast in, fast out. '

Officer Zheng compromised.

'You wait for me outside. '

Yang Ru said to Gu chang zch.

Officer Zheng knows it very well—although Yang Ru is tricky, he is quite clever,

Let him inspect the case, it is very helpful to solve it.

About ten minutes later, Yang Ru walks out from the inside with a smile.

Officer Zheng wants to ask something to him ...

Yang Rui just pats his shoulder, says:

'Thanks a lot, Officer Zheng. '

'Contact again. '

Then, he takes Gu chang zch and hurries away.

They sit down at an open —air cafe.

'You will be too tired, '

'You have to look for a "red jade talisman"and help police catch the murder. '

Gu chang zch said to Yang Ru ; He knew what Officer Zheng
expected.

'They are compossible. '

Yang Ru replied easily.

'You see my two major discoveries! '

Yang Ru adjusts the mobile phone screen, moves to Gu chang zch.

An image of a pink gauze hood lamp reflects in Gu chang zch's
eyes.

'I just say it is romantic. '

Gu chang zch lazily answered.

'It is true that it is romantic! '

Yang Rui smiled.

'However, it is not for decoration or lighting, '

'It may be the place to hide the"red jade talisman"! '

His eyebrows were raised.

'I went in and observed. '

'Found that the lampshade has a very fine red line! '

'My great grand father had mentioned, '

'The"red jade talisman"was wrapped with a white silk which has
red patterns. '

'So you doubt...'

'The red line was fall from the"red jade talisman"...'

'Murder killed owner, also stole it. '

Gu chang zch went on to say.

'And this...'

Yang Ru showed another picture to him.

'Is it a trade mark of certain product? '

Gu chang zch stared at a gold star logo, was not sure.

'But its hanging wire is longer, '

'It should be a luggage tag. '

'This is general practice. '

'If a person kills someone, he must flee abroad first. '

'It is more stable to book flight ticket and hotel in advance. '

'Some very top hotels would send the thanks letter and a few small items with hotel logo to the subscriber before he or she checks in. '

'If we can find out a hotel with the gold star logo and live in it. '

'It is very likely that the murder will be caught. '

Yang Ru analyzed all way.

'The police officer treated the luggage tag as garbage, '

'But it is just a useful garbage for us. '

He proudly said.

'I am afraid it is not easy to find it. '

Gu chang zch doubted.

'I am internet ranger. '

'Operate an online store. '

'Always search the web. '

'There must be gains. '

Yang Ru was very confident.

Then, he gathers his hair, puts his hands in his trouser pockets,

Mains his free and easy appearance.

Yang Ru was almost crazy about searching the internet, also asked several travel agencies.

But they just met the trademarks of many hotels, didn't find any hotel with the gold star logo.

'Maybe we should turn a direction. '

'For example, '

'Visit Officer Zheng, get some other clues. '

Gu chang zch advised Yang Ru.

Mobile phone is ring.

Gu chang zch picks up it.

'Hello, uncle…'

'Are you coming to Taipei? '

'We will go to" orchid"tea restaurant to meet. '

'Yes, at Xingyang Street. '

'See you later. '

He puts down the phone, places his hand on Yang Ru' s shoulder, speaks softly:

'I go out for a while. '

'Don't always wander around the little star. '

'Time to relax.'

'I am so sorry, uncle. '

'You are far from the south. '

'I just meet you in this small shop. '

Gu chang zch said so, because this Huande uncle is a gourmet.

He even left for Macao to taste the Michelin five star dinners.

Flied to Tokyo to enjoy expensive sushi.

'Although it is a small shop, '

'Foods are flavorful. '

  Lee Huande gives Gu chang zch a slight smile, has a drink of milk

tea and takes a bite of coconut sauce toast.

'I am glad to hear uncle saying that. '

Gu chang zch sincerely said.

There is a feeling in his eyes.

In childhood wandering time,

He went to various relatives to taken turns to be a guest, this uncle

Huande treated him best.

So far, they still keep in touch with each other.

Gu chang zch's eyes shows affection for Lee Huande deeply.

Lee Huande looks at the nephew who is also his half son.

The skin is a little black, but the appearance is still not too bad!

Handsome eyebrows and eyes, strong body, width shoulder.

Just the fate is a little bit worse.

'Last time, I heard your voice was wrong on the phone. '

'Is every thing all right, now? '

Lee Huande was concerned about Gu chang zch.

'It was passed. '

Gu chang zch took a breath of air.

He can not let uncle know that he wanted to end himself recently.

'You are still young. '

'There are many changes in the future. '

'Some setbacks were actually revelations. '

'Can be used as a cornerstone for future development.'

Lee Huande did his best to encourage his nephew.

'The kind of longan candy that you loved when you were a child.'

'I bring you some. '

He opened the suitcase.

This makes Gu chang zch stunned!

Not for the box of beautifully wrapped candy.

But a folder next to it!

The train pattern on top of the folder, there is the 'gold star. ' mark on locomotive!

'That is the souvenir I got on the Japanese " Gold Star" train. '

'You stared fixed at it...'

'Must be quite interested in this thing.'

'So I give it to you. '

Lee Huande generously stated, handed the folder to Gu chang zch.

'It turns out that we are not going to live in a hotel but to take a train. '

Yang Ru held the folder with the gold star sigh, said.

'According to uncle Huande's statement, '

'The " Gold Star" train has not yet officially opened. '

'So we won't find it. '

'At this trial sale stage, '

'The train is still extremely difficulty to order. '

'Uncle Huande is a tea merchant, often does business with

Japanese people. '

'He got on the" Gold Star"train ...'

'Relied on the special relationship of these Japanese customers.'

Gu chang zch was not optimistic about taking the' Gold Star' train.

'Do you trust me? '

Yang Ru asked Gu chang zch.

'Leave your passport with me. '

'And don't worry, just have a good time! '

'We will be a thrill train journey in the future. '

Yang Ru' s attitude was firm.

Gu chang zch listens to Yang Ru' s words completely.

The next few days...

He wanders the street shops and played video games without

restrictions.

However, on the other side of his heart,

He just thinks that Yang Ru is just doing one thing, they may be not

really take the' Gold Star' train.

But in a rainy afternoon...

Gu chang zch is just playing the computer game'The monkey king'.

Yang Ru' s phone is coming.

'Prepare one week's baggage. '

'8: 00 tomorrow morning,meet at Eva Air Aviation counter. '

'Take the plane at ten am. '

'Go to Fukuoka, Japan. '

'Seven days and six night the Kyushu " Gold Star" train journey established. '

Yang Ru gave Gu chang zch a concise instruction.

Part two

Japan amazing train trip

The day before taking the train,

Yang Ru andGu chang zch stay at the Grand Hyatty hotel for one

night.

The lobby of the hotel is just facing a large shopping mall"Canal

City Hakata".

At this moment,

Yang Ru is sitting in the lobby.

Chews the mints, looks at the mall outside the window.

Gu chang zch is murmuring at the side.

'You did not say an word along the way. '

'Just sleep! sleep! sleep! '

'Now, you actually become a gloomy literary youth. '

'Always stare at outside the window. '

'I don't want to follow you like a headless fly in Japan. '

'You must tell me something. '

'How did you book " Gold Star" train? '

Gu chang zch impolitely pulled Yang Ru's sleeve and said.

'Your uncle has the Japanese customers. '

'I have a godmother who is the president of railway fan club. '

Yang Ru replied faintly.

'"Grand Hyatty" was a quite, isolated hotel originally, '

'"Canal City Hakata"is opened, '

'The noise is coming in. '

'The atmosphere of the entire hotel has changed. '

'It's like...'

He bits his low lip, then, says:

'A guest who takes part in the" Gold Star" train journey is to enjoy a private time in a secret space. '

'But we join it, '

'Turn it into a journey of trouble! '

Yang Ru had no way out.

'You said that we are going to stir up trouble. '

Gu chang zch reclined on the couch, said languidly.

'Actually, I have locked one of passengers. '

'Who is it? '

Gu chang zch heard Yang Ru say this, jumped up the coach and shouted.

' My godmother who is the president of railway fan club. '

'My godfather just is the major shareholder of the" Gold Star" train. '

'So I can check the passengers list and their information first. '

Yang Ru stopped here,did not continue to say.

'You just did not want to say more. '

Gu chang zch complained.

'Be calm…'

'After getting on the train, it is not too late to leak it to you. '

Yang Ru patted Gu chang zch's hand, said .

'This journey will require a lot of brainpower and strength. '

'We need some great food! '

'Let's Forget all troubles. '

'Just enjoy the Japanese style"Peking duck". '

Yang Ru drags Gu chang zch to the hotel's Chinese restaurant.

On the next morning,

They attend the' Gold Star'train' s welcome party in the special room of the train station.

After drinking a few glasses of fruit wine,

Passengers pass the exclusive passage of this train,enter the rooms inside the carriage.

When Yang Ru and Gu chang zch get into the room,

Gu chang zch can't help screaming!

It is an ultra—elegant suit!

Dark coffee tones.

The sofa which is red plum pattern on white,is put the shinny, soft silk chair pillows.

Hollowed out screen, three layers curtaln.

'No way!'

'We ordered the" Gold Star" train too late. '

'Just received the top suit.'

Yang Ru played the curved design on the lamppost, answered.

' You wasted too much money...'

Gu chang zch has not finished his words yet, the doorbell rings.

Yang Ru opens the door.

A middle—age woman stands outside!

Bright red lips, thick mascara, puts on blue and white tulle dress.

Under long curl hair, she wears a pair of earrings in the shape of a torch.

'Excuse me...'

She deeply bowed, spoke Japanese.

'My name is Kaneko. '

'I am a bar keeper at Shibuya. '

'There are a lot of Taiwanese to come to my store. '

'So, I can speak a little Chinese. '

Kaneko circled thumb and index finger, means 'less', introduced herself with less influent Chinese.

'May I come in and visit? '

She asked.

'Please. '

Yang Ru made a gesture.

'I heard it early...'

'The train has a top suit. '

'Originally, I wanted to stay it. '

'But thought about it later...'

'Living alone, it's too big, too wasteful. '

'So I decided to just visit it. '

Kaneko starts looking around in the room.

'The room is not big enough. '

'Hanging woodcut is also dull. '

She glanced at a gold flower woodcut on the wall.

'How are the sleepers so narrow? '

'Like two noodles. '

'As train shakes, '

'You will sleep more uncomfortable. '

She saw two single beds on bed room through the opened
compartment door, called.

Gu chang zch has already become impatient with the babbler.

Yang Ru just smiled and keeps manner.

But his eyes are always staring at her.

'After visiting, '

'I feel enough. '

'Think no more of this suit. '

Kaneko exhaled a breath out.

'Sorry to bother you. '

She deeply bowed once again.

'Don't you see it more? '

Yang Ru politely asked her.

'No, thanks.'

'See you in the dinner. '

'We can sit together. '

Kaneko smiled seductively.

'Good— bye, handsome guy!'

She waved to Yang Ru, then, steps out of the room.

'What is wrong with the woman? '

When Kaneko left, Gu chang zch can't wait to ask his partner.

'Her earrings...'

'One of" Seven elites in Tao faction"—Ning Yuhua...'

'I had seen her portrait which my grand great father painted. '

'She worn a pair of earrings just like Kaneko's. '

'Torch was just the mark of" Seven elites in Tao faction"! '

'It turns out that you had been attention to her earrings! '

Gu chang zch suddenly realized.

'I had mentioned" Ning Yuhua married early to go abroad. '

'And she just married to Japan. '

'So you suspect that Kaneko is the descendant of Ning Yuhua? '

Gu chang zch asked nervously.

'Just suspect...'

'May be this is a coincidence. '

'Tow women worn the same earrings. '

Yang Ru's attitude suddenly turn to ease.

'Had you heard the Japanese song"The clock of Nagasaki"? '

'No, I only had eat" Nagasaki cake". '

Gu chang zch replied in a funny way.

'Whether it is for the clock or the cake, '

'The train is approaching Nagasaki. '

'We can go down and have a fun. '

'Don't hurry back for lunch. '

Yang Ru made a gesture of stopping.

'Only dinner, all guests will arrive. '

They strolled around in Nagasaki.

Gave up lunch, but tasted a high— grade afternoon tea.

Yang Ru is leisurely and carefree.

Gu chang zch is just anxious...

He really wants know who are these people in the same train?

Who is the Yang Ru's target person?

He can't wait to come to dinner at six o'clock to get clear

understanding.

It is hard to get to half past five.

They wear suits, ties, put on formal clothing.

Pass through the art atmosphere carriages which are full of

paintings...

Go in the dining room arranged into starry sky.

Some one has been sitting there!

He gives Gu chang zch and Yang Ru a friendly smile, says:

'My name is Yamada Hikaru. '

'You are Mr. Yang and Mr. Gu, from Taiwan, right? '

'I heard the stuff on the train mentioned you. '

'Would you like to sit with me? '

So the three of them converse with each other while drinking aperitif.

Yamada says he is a business man selling ceramics.

In addition to domestic market,

Also opens up market in Southeast Asia.

He often goes to Taiwan.

Therefore, he can not only speak Mandarin but also a little bit of Taiwanese.

Really like Alishan, Longshan temple, Hualian...these places, had traveled many times.

'In this way, you have to endure my strange Chinese. '

Yamada ridiculed himself.

'How could be...'

Gu chang zch and Yang Ru said in unison.

'I carry a few paper weights. '

'Give them to people that I met on the trip. '

'Now, I send them to you as souvenirs. '

Yamada take out two rectangular boxes.

They open them:

A paper weight is placed in each box ; there is a very detailed gold pattern on it.

Gu chang zch and Yang Ru are quite happy to accept his gifts.

Their emotions are also very cheerful!

And believe they will have a lucky train journey!

A short haired girl with big eyes approaches their table.

'How are you doing? '

'My name is Kagegawa Kazuko. '

'I am responsible for piano playing on the train. '

'We have the rule. '

'Each guest can chose one of their favorite songs and give it to me to play. '

She handed over several pieces of music scores.

'Are you Mr. Yang and Mr. Gu? '

Her eyes fell on Gu chang zch and Yang Ru.

'My great—grand mother was from Taiwan too. '

'She even had learned Chinese Taoism. '

'And I studied Mandarin in Peking by myself. '

Then, Kazuko showed a few blunt Mandarin.

When Yang Ru would like to ask more about Kazuko's great—grand mother...

Kaneko hurries up into dinning room like a gust of wind!

Earrings still, her clothes are just replaced by black and orange dinner dress.

Holding Kazuko, she touches the earrings for a while, points to the clothes for a while ...says a series of words.

Yang Ru gets to focus, tries to understand her in his limited Japanese.

Kazuko sees this situation, then, explains it to him with Mandarin:

'Kaneko said she really loves the earrings I sent her. '

'They are stylish, match her dress tonight. '

she adds another supplement:

'The thing was my special order. '

'The torch pattern is from my great—grand mother. '

Yang Ru and Gu chang zch become suddenly aware of:

' Ning Yuhua's descendent has another person! '

'Sorry, I change my mind. '

'I want to be alone, sitting next to the piano. '

'Enjoy Kazuko's performance well. '

'We became friends regardless of the age difference. '

Kaneko said to Yang Ru and Gu chang zch.

'But it seems that you have found a companion. '

Kaneko looked at Yamada.

Yamada politely raised himself slightly.

'Then, have a wonderful night! '

She waves to them and walks to piano.

Kazuko is taking musical scores of passengers' chosen songs, preparing at the piano.

The passengers in the train have continued to enter the dining room.

A newly married couple who have honey moon, are sitting at corner.

Two heads next to each other, are occupied with endless whisper of love.

An old couple about six years old, are sitting in silence.

Slowly drink the crystal red sherry.

There is a family of four.

Parents and a pair of children that are about fifteen, sixteen years old ,make a noise.

  At this time, A short young man is close to Yang Ru and Gu chang zch's table.

'It is great to meet friends from Taiwan on the train! '

'I can hear a lot of interesting things from foreign country to broaden horizon. '

'I am full of enthusiasm about that! '

'May I join you? '

Young man spoke with English.

Sees every one has no objection, he also joins the conversation.

Young man says his name is Kataoka akita, is a chopper salesman.

Then, he begins to rattle on...

  Emphasizes that chopper is real a soul of dish!

If the material are not cut well, how to make delicious food?

With a chopper, it is greatly learned!

Killing fish, slicing meat, cutting cheese...you have to choose the chopper carefully, never be sloppy .

Moves all his professional knowledge out!

Next, he talks about his 'marketing glorious history'.

Set up a stall at festival.

He sold out more than one hundred choppers in an hour.

The housewives also rushed to ask him for signatures and photos.

Just like a super star!

Kataoka is enraptured, can't stop talking.

Gu chang zch wonders in his heart:

'Doesn't the chopper salesman want to hear something from aboard?

'But how does he always talk about himself? '

He casts a double glance at Yang Ru.

Yang Ru just smiles, dosen't take it seriously.

He seems to say:

'What does it matter to hear someone bragging? '

The lights have been dimmed.

A beautiful melody comes!

Kazuko is playing the song which passenger ordered.

So everyone listen quietly in a moment.

Dishes come one after another...

Cold cuts, salads, main courses, deserts...The chef took a mixing cooking method, full used of Kyushu special local products: pork, sweet potatoes, chestnuts...

The plum wine and ginger sodas used to match meals are the same.

A last male passenger is sitting alone.

Bronze skin, poker face has no feeling.

Looks completely different from the group.

Gu chang zch notices that Yang Ru secretly observes the male passenger.

He is about more than forty years old.

Judging by his limbs and body type, Gu chang zch thinks he should study material art. There is a nine—square bento placed in front of the male passenger.

A variety of different boiled foods are put in it ； To fu, potato, plum, wasabi, burdock, black soybean...and a glutinous rice ball that they had never seen it.

'Why is the man eating another food？'

Yang Ru pointed at the male passenger's bento, asked the waiter with English and Japanese.

'That is special request of Mr.Miyazaki.'

The waiter answered with pure English.

'He asked for a light diet ； no sugar, no oil, and no strong taste.'

'There is a kind glutinous rice ball mixed with honey and wine.'

'It was very troublesome to make it.'

He grins:

'But this is the spirit of the train— meets all customers' needs.'

'"Light diet", "glutinous rice ball"...'

Waiting for the waiter to leave, Yang Ru muttered to himself, was very concerned about the two things.

After Kazuko played a few world famous songs and Japanese folk songs, she just stops playing temporarily.

Magic show begins!
A man who is dressed as an Indian magician.
He puts on a show ; swallows fire, silk scarf knotted, the cigarette case is gone...
They are just general magic tricks.
But everyone applauds widely.
Gu chang zch also calls a few times to vent the depression in his chest.

The magic show came to end.
Piano performance begins again!
Kazuko plays the elegant 'Moon Light Sonata'.
Everybody reveals the expression of well—being intoxicated.
Yamada is half turned, Kataoka is slightly sideways...
They have become one— to —one intimate conversation.
Ceramic merchant and chopper salesman seem to have a lot of experience to exchange.
Gu chang zch continues to observe Mr.Miyazaki.

He sits upright.

There is still no emotion on his face.

'Presumably, these performances did not resonate with him. '

Gu chang zch surmised.

All at once,

There is a killing in Miyazaki's eyes!

Gu chang zch quickly turns his eyes away.

The romantic atmosphere around has disappeared!

He has a sense of crisis!

Gu chang zch gazes at outside the window…

Haze mountains, sea, flowers, trees are in the dark as phantoms.

He is shocked!

'Mr.Miyazaki is your target person, right? '

Ended dinner, back the room, Gu chang zch immediately asked.

'I have investigated, '

Yang Ru took off his suit and said slowly.

'Miyazaki is a flower farmer from Mie—Ken. '

'Mie—Ken is just Japanese ninjas' home land. '

'Miyazaki leaked secrets in his diet on the dinner. '

'The ninja avoids getting fat and can do a quick jump with the light diet. '

'Does not let the body emit strong smell so that people can not find his exact whereabouts.'

'This is the way the ninja must keep eating. '

'Glutinous rice ball mixed with honey and wine. '

'It is the Bing long ball that the ninja must carry with the task. '

'I see the killing in his eyes. '

Gu chang zch said.

'Although Miyazaki has been in the middle age, '

'His skin is moist and light. '

'His limbs are slender and strong. '

'This is the result of his training from a ninja! '

Yang Ru analyzed Miyazaki again.

'Do you suspect that he is Yuan Zhi Jian's descendent? '

'But his surname is Miyazaki, not Yuan. '

Gu chang zch was puzzled.

'May be he is from mother's surname. '

'And the name can be changed anytime. '

Yang Ru explained.

'After this dinner, '

'I suspect another person. '

Yang Ru meditated.

'You mean" Kazuko '? '

'She is not like a ferocious person. '

Gu chang zch remembered that her fingers were leap on the keyboard, pure and dexterous.

'Had you read news? '

Yang Ru cried.

'Do not all female spies have innocent and flawless appearance? '

'Deceive the people's eyes and ears to achieve the goals! '

'In short, '

Gu chang zch said, his eyes are almost closed.

'You and me should not presuppose the position first. '

'Except for Miyazaki and Kazuko, '

'We must carefully observe every one on the train. '

'This meal was real tired...'

'Like a hunter waiting for his prey bitterly. '

Finishing the talking, Gu chang zch goes bed, turns over and falls asleep.

Yang Ru has no sleepiness, sitting the edge of the bed.

With the rhythm of the train bumps,

He keeps thinking.

Gu chang zch mentioned the' prey. '...

He will also track the'prey ' tomorrow!

Yang Ru sees that Gu chang zch sleeps soundly by the side of him.

He thoughtfully dims the desk lamp.

The next morning,

The train stops Yufuin.

There are a variety of local products shop near the station in it.

Passengers can take off the train and stroll around.

Yang Ru turns into the housewife this tlme.

Yang Ru and Gu chang zch follows Miyazaki one after the other.

Yang Ru stares at Miyazaki but he completely shows the way a house wife is shopping.

This makes Gu chang zch feel a little bit admire:

'The sly boy is not only good at disguising himself but also perfect acting! '

Miyazaki wears a purple shirt, tall figure, is very eye—catching in the crowd.

He doesn't go shopping just like a tourist.

He is rushing forward...

Walks as if on wings, not be out of breath or even fainting flushed face.

It is a super light Kung Fu!

Yang Ru and Gu chang zch more believe that Miyazaki is a well trained ninja.

In a flash...

Their eyes on Miyazaki have turned from appreciation to horror!

Dozens of fine needles fly like raindrops...

Cast to Miyazaki.

Their 'prey' has fallen to the ground!

The ' Gold Star' train stop driving in Yufuin.

Miyazaki was assassinated here!

The local police takes translator to carefully interrogated

passengers and employees in the train.

Yang Ru and Gu chang zch become extremely important

eyewitnesses.

They are asked more than others.

A dreamy train journey has cast a shadow!

Every one gets a little down.

After a few hours of investigation by police.

   Train re—stars!

Delayed afternoon tea becomes a feast that gets over a shock.

In the dining room...

Every one is free to order coffee, tea, juice to go with three tier

snack tray .

Gu chang zch watches out the reaction of each passenger.

The old couple are still as calm as ever.

Enjoy refreshment gracefully.

The newly married couple is still sitting at corner

Two heads next to each other, are occupied with endless whisper

of love.

It seems that murder had never happened.

But the family of four is no longer noisy.

Quietly eating and drinking.

Gu chang zch, Yang Ru, Yamada, Kaneko, and Kataoka sit together.

Kaneko and Kataoka comment on the murder with mixcd

language ：Japanese, Chinese and English.

'You must not take ill. '

'I am so indifferent to this case. '

'Just because I see too much.'

'In the street of my store, blood events often occur. '

'But my store has always been safe. '

'I am tactful in deal with people. '

'No matter how much I am not happy, '

'I have to smile. '

She opened her lips and made a smile.

'For business, I must protect myself. '

Kaneko drunk a cup of tea with a lot of milk, said in the tone of self—confidence.

'I did not have any intersection with Miyazaki on the train. '

'The police said that he is farming. '

'I see him like a villain. '

'I had a Taiwanese guest who said "You shall pay what you have done. ". '

'Miyazaki just "paid "! '

Kaneko looks around everybody for advice.

Everybody has nothing to say about her words.

Gu chang zch just comprehends that the killing of Miyazaki's eyes was pointing to himself!

'In fact, '

'I am the one that is most relevant to this case! '

Kataoka unexpectedly popped up such a sentence.

'I didn't say that I killed Miyazaki. '

Saw every one's panic, he corrected his words immediately.

'I am a chopper salesman. '

'I also have research on other types knives. '

'The police who asked questions mentioned, '

'The lethal weapon was many delicate needles. '

Kataoka takes a sip of bitter, strong coffee, the facial expression is
  solemnly. The spirit of every one is concentrated on the term
  'lethal weapon'.

'However, it should not be a needle but a knife. '

'"Willow leaf knife"!'

'Very, very fine knife...'

'The knife was coated with poison. '

'The poison is called "Thousand layer cream"! '

' More a dozen of knives fly out at the same time, '

He made a flying knife action to enhance the effect.

'The target person is killed presently. '

'And there is no chance of even a cure! '

Yang Ru has studied some Japanese material art factions, but
never heard of 'Willow leaf knife'!

'"Willow leaf knife"is a specific use of a family! '

When every one wanted to know more about 'Willow leaf knife',
Kataoka just made a conclusion in this statement.

'Mr. Kataoka...'

Yamada said quietly.

'You didn't see corpse and lethal weapon with your own eyes. '

''Willow leaf knife' can be regarded as your personal assumption. '

'I didn't say the thing must be like that...'

  Kataoka scratched his head, admitted with some embarrassment.

'Just gave opinions for every one's reference. '

'But may be it is right? '

He made a funny face.

'Any way, '

'May the dead rest in peace.'

Yamada bend his head and said lowly.

The words came out...

Every one becomes extraordinarily quiet.

The afternoon tea thus comes to an end.

Although a murder occurred,

The train was still in accordance with the scheduled itinerary.

Went to Oita, Miyakonojo, Kagoshima...these places.

Passengers were not comfortable this with unexpected incident
though.

They still covered the distance.

Yummy foods, beautiful scenery, special products...didn't miss
anything .

On the night before the train is going back to Hakata,

Gu chang zch and Yang Ru pack their luggages in the room.

Yang Ru suddenly wants to buy a towel with gold star logo to

commemorate.

He goes to the gift department on the train.

When he comes back, happens to meet Yamada who walks out of

the room.

'Mr. Yang...'

He greeted him.

'You and Mr. Gu made a special trip to take the train from abroad. '

'But met the killing, '

'And greatly reduced the pleasure of travel.'

'I represent my country, '

'Solemnly apologize for you. '

Yamada made a deep bow to Yang Ru.

'I don't deserve it. '

Yang Ru also bowed back.

'Mr. Yamada，'

' You didn't say that。'

'The train journey still has many things and people that are

unforgettable. '

'For example, '

'You, Mr. Yamada.'

His words just finished,

The body of the train suddenly becomes unstable and goes straight ahead.

Yang Ru almost falls, but fortunately, Yamada helps him in time .

'Your internal strength is so strong! '

Yang Ru said, gazed on Yamada with amazement.

Doll, fan, protective talisman, Kusamochi...

Gu chang zch arranged these local products for appreciation.

'We did not know whereabouts of the murder and the ' red jade talisman' in this Japan train tour...'

'But there are these local products that can be brought back. '

'This can be barely counted as a harvest! '

He said to Yang Ru who just entered.

'Not really, '

Yang Ru replied.

'There are a lot of things. '

'But the paper weights Mr. Yamada sent us are the most delicate and interesting! '

Gu chang zch takes paper weight from the duffel bag and plays it.

It seems to be influenced by Gu chang zch.

Yang Ru also finds his own paper weight.

'Mr. Yamada is the best person I have encountered on this trip. '

'He is cautious and moderate. '

'Knows how to get along with people.'

'Still is very humorous, talkative. '

'We are comfortable and at ease with him. '

'He reminds me of uncle Huande. '

'After returning to Taiwan, '

'I will miss him. '

Gu chang zch said to himself.

And Yang Ru was not listening。

He clasps the paper weight.

And his fingertips are almost stuck in the golden patterns on it.

His eyes condense and his facial lines are tightening.

Gu chang zch sees that Yang Ru seems to think about a difficulty problem.

'This problem should be related to ' red jade talisman' and the murder who killed Yan Chenzhao or Miyazaki. '

Gu chang zch guessed.

'As Yang Ru' s word"not really"…'

'Maybe our tracking is about to start, not end! '

Gu chang zch judged secretly.

Therefore, he is determined not to bother Yang Ru any more.

He puts away those local products,

Returns to the work on packing luggage.

After the gold star train held a farewell party in the special room of the train station,

Passengers are divided into two types:

Some people get out of the station and they part ways.

Others stay in the Grand Hyatty hotel again.

Such as Gu chang zch, Yang Ru, Yamada Hikaru and the family of four.

Seven people ride to the hotel together.

Gu chang zch sizes the last chance and keeps talking to Yamada.

He also notices that Yang Ru is more aware of Yamada's every movement.

When they arrives at hotel,

Gu chang zch and Yang Ru asks Yamada and the family of four check in first.

The counter staff seems to be more intimate to Yamada than other guests.

Gu chang zch thinks Yamada should be a frequent visitor to this hotel.

Yang Ru vaguely hears with his limited Japanese that Yamada had booked a restaurant.

Gu chang zch and Yang Ru see intentionally or unintentionally the counter staff wrote on the paper:

'Moon Kiosk, 7pm. '

'Moon Kiosk' is famous for its Kaiseki cuisine.

It has many tatami rooms.

Guest can dine in room without being bothered.

Also can invite performer to play shamisen in it.

Yamada walks through the elegant garden under guidance of the waiter...

Comes to the inmost room.

After entering,

Yamada sits cross legged.

He didn't have a set meal.

But a few small dishes of appetizers ; roasted king crab legs, vinegar cod liver, pickled scallops...and a pot of hot sake.

While waiting for the dishes,

He begins to appreciate the room named 'Sakura Dance'.

Its space is quite spacious and may be more suitable for meetings.

Beauty painting and banana painting are hung on the wall.

There are also flowers arrangements and lacquer wares.

Everything in the room is pleasing to the eyes!

When he and she came 'Moon Kiosk',

They often designated this room.

Although he had to spend more money,

It could make her feel refreshed and have a wonderful meal!

Yamada takes out a hairpin from his bosom.

He can't stop touching it.

There seems to be endless love and thoughts hidden it.

In an instant...

The paper door is opened.

It is Yang Ru!

'Mr. Yang...'

'I have been expecting you. '

Yamada was not too surprised.

Yang Ru sits down on the tatami.

Then, he stares at Yamada with anticipation.

'Last night, '

'I heard you say" Your internal strength is so strong! "on the train. '

'I just understood that you knew it. '

Yamada smiled softly, the tone was steady, not hurry.

'When checking in at the hotel, '

'I found you glanced at the note"Moon Kiosk, 7pm. ". '

'So I thought that you will follow me here. '

His attitude is always calm.

Sake and dishes are delivered.

Yamada asks the waiter to add more table ware.

The table ware is quickly sent.

Yamada pours sake for Yang Ru.

'There is some thing. '

Yang Ru was a little hesitant.

'Before Miyazaki was killed, '

'I saw a view of back on the street that was very similar to yours. '

'I had never told anyone about this, '

'Including the police who came to ask questions and my partner.'

He looks straight at Yamada, has a sip of sake.

'I always respect you very much, Mr. Yamada. '

'You are generous and noble. '

'Take care of us a lot. '

'I would rather my double about you is wrong. '

Yang Ru said honestly.

'The paper weight that you gave me, '

'The patterns above it...'

'At first sight, '

'They look like willow leaves. '

'But keep a close watch on them, '

'Their shapes are sharper and thinner than average willow leaves. '

'So the patterns are not the willow leaves but the knives. '

'Knife!'

'"Willow leaf knife" Kataoka said! '

Yamada has no reaction, just catches a piece of cod liver with great taste.

'Under the violent shaking of the train, '

'You could hold me without being affected. '

'This proved that you have a strong internal force. '

'Only such a person can launch"Willow leaf knives"so accurately, '

'And let people die. '

'I also used a little personal relationship, '

'Investigated the background information of train passengers.'

Yang Ru' s face was slightly hot.

He felt that he seemed to be spying on the privacy of others.

'You and Miyazaki are just from Mie—Ken— ninja's home land. '

'You and him are all from the ninja family. '

'Both of you are the highly skilled ninja, right? '

Yang Ru sees that Yamada did not deny it, he further questions:

'In the Tao world of China, '

'There was a combination called "Seven elites in Tao faction". '

'One of the members called Yuan Zhi Jian. '

'He was born in Japan ninja family. '

'Are you a descendant of him? '

'It is right that I am from a ninja family. '

'But my family name is Yamada, not Yuan. '

After Yamada quickly answered,

He picks up the wine pot, pours sake for himself and Yang Ru.

'Cheers! '

Yamada raised his porcelain cup.

'I am afraid there will be no such opportunity in the future! '

He seemed to say good bye to Yang Ru.

Yang Ru can't help but shock.

Yang Ru just obeys to toast with him.

'Today's Yamada, '

'Every one says that he is a nice person! '

Yamada put down the porcelain cup, laughed at himself.

'I was not like this before...'

He stroked his forehead.

'Taking advantage of my extraordinary family and not weak Kung

Fu, '

'I was bloated with pride. '

'Indulged in sensual pleasure.'

'Often fought with people.'

'I had no regret, '

'Instead, I felt that was a marvelous thing to dominate between

heaven and earth! '

'Finally, '

'The retribution was coming. '

His head hung low, spoke in thin voice.

'Too frequently enter and exit red—light districts, '

'I got leprosy! '

Yang Ru stars at the gentle, perfect ceramic merchant with surprise.

'The disease will make people' s facial features change, skin

ulcerate...

 ''Gradually, '

'Even the nerves will paralyze. '

'My whole spirit had collapsed! '

'So I imprisoned myself in a broken, dirty apartment, '

'Was isolated from all friends and relatives.'

'Prepared to die!'

'At this time, '

'There was a woman. '

Yamada's face was soft, dreamlike.

'She was the maid of my family, '

'Came from Taiwan.'

'I rarely went home. '

'Even if I went back, '

'I had never noticed her...'

'Thought of her as air.'

Yamada reproaches himself, snorts coldly.

'And she actually came to my residence, just simply said: '

'"I will take care of you. ". '

'I yelled at her rudely: '

'"I am nothing to you. ". '

'"You do this, What are your purpose? ". '

'She told me something...'

'Her sister wanted to have a surgery in Taiwan. '

'Needed a sum of money.'

'My parents happened to be out for travel. '

'No one could borrow money for her. '

'I was just at home, '

'Gave her a limited edition brand watch.'

'Sold it into cash.'

'Solved this difficulty.'

'She said she owed me a favor. '

'And I deliberated answered her: '

'"I was not interesting in helping a maid. ". '

'"Just because I already tired of this watch, ". '

'"Looked at it unsightly. ". '

'"Hoped some one would take it away quickly. ". '

Yang Ru smiles quietly,

He thinks Yamada's statement was very ingenious.

'She still insisted on staying. '

'Made the bed and folded the quilts. '

'Sweeped and cooked.'

'I didn't want to go to doctor, '

'She brought the doctor to the apartment, '

'Let me take medicine, rub medicine. '

'At first few days, '

'I kept humiliating her. '

'Punched and kicked her. '

Yamada can not help sighing and sobbing constantly.

'She only silently endured every thing. '

'Did what she thought she should do. '

'Once, '

'I pointed at my festering face, roared at her:

'"Leprosy is terminal ill. ". '

'"Terminal ill! ". '

'"You care about me. ". '

'"I do not appreciate you at all. ". '

'" You will only be infected to death. ". '

'You can't think I used to be such a beast, right? '

Yamada asked Yang Ru.

'It is unbelievable! '

He replied in a fine voice.

'She was staring at me tightly, said:

'"Didn't heal until end…". '

'"How do you know the result? ". '

'Her eyes were so affectionated and determined! '

'The tremendous power they emitted was enough to devour the soul of a person. '

'I just looked at her for along time without saying a word. '

'Since then, '

'My attitude had converged. '

Yamada flatten his voice.

'I don't know if she touched God or I was forgiven, '

'My illness had gradually improved. '

'Finally, '

'I recovered to the original me! '

He said gratefully .

Yamada is still deeply immersed in the past .

'Escaped from this catastrophe, '

'My temperament had changed a lot. '

'Became a well regulated ceramic businessman.'

He smiled relievedly.

Yamada calls the waiter to add wine.

Fills himself's and Yang Ru' s porcelain cups with sake again.

His whole person seems to be alive one more time!

'You and her?...'

Yang Ru tentatively asked.

'She and me are not only just lovers. '

'She gave me a new life. '

'I regard her as the master and god. '

'In Japan, '

'We have so called" ninja's soul". '

'Ninja must not only have excellent skills, '

'He has to be completely responsible for his master. '

'She is my master. '

'So I am willing to make any sacrifice for her. '

Yamada cautiously expressed.

'"Make any sacrifice for her. ". '

Yang Ru carefully recalled this sentence.

'I once found a luggage tag with gold star next to a corpse. '

'Then, tracked the train up.'

'The dead was called Yan Chenzhao. '

'He was the owner of'Hui qui 'appliance shop. '

'Was that luggage tag which you dropped? '

Yang Ru looked directly at him and asked.

'You just asked if I am a descendant of"Seven elites in Tao faction"...'

'I am not, '

'But she is. '

Yamada lowered his head and said thoughtfully .

Yang Ru is surprised and look at Yamada uncertainly.

'From her, '

'I knew a lot about "Seven elites in Tao faction". '

'Six of them were good at Taoism! '

'Everyone was arrogant and proud of the crowd! '

'They were all outstanding and brilliant! '

'Only except, '

'He Lei!'

Yang Ru followed his words.

'Yes, He Lei...'

'He had no achievements in Taoism. '

'Just was a silly clown. '

'Was despised and insulted.'

'The master of"Seven elites in Tao faction"— Wu Tia nji held the

Taoist ultimate treasure—"red jade talisman"! '

Yamada got a little rusty at the term 'red jade talisman'.

Yang Ru twitches his shoulder unconsciously.

'He Lei thought Wu Tia nji would give "red jade talisman"to his favorite disciple— Wu Hao ying in a secret way. '

'But in the end, '

'The "red jade talisman "would fall in Li Yan's or Yan changrong's hands. '

'After all, '

'They are most ambitious people in "Seven elites in Tao faction"! '

'No one expected, '

'This silly clown had made up his mind that he must win the "red jade talisman"! '

'May be after a few generations, '

'The"red jade talisman' should belong to his family finally! '

Yamada said hard as if he had a kind of burden.

'It is weird! '

'He Lei was the most worth person to watch out! '

Yang Ru floated a strange, faint sad smile and said.

'She heard her grandfather's things and wish from her father, '

'And she had the same experience as her grandfather. '

' Also had been hurt and bullied. '

Yamada said heavily.

'This strengthened her determination to win "red jade talisman"
  for her grandfather!'

'However, various life experience made her be smart and
confident. '

'Eliminated the feeling of inferiority.'

His face showed admiration.

'She kept track of Li Yan's and Yan changrong's descendants from
time to time. '

'She had visited 'Hui qui 'appliance shop many times. '

'But nothing.'

'Until there was a late night, '

'She was at a distance from "Hui qui" appliance shop...'

'Saw a colorful light coming out of it. '

'She knew that it was the light which "red jade talisman' shines
every ten years. '

'So the next day, '

'She went to the"Hui qui "appliance shop as a customer again. '

'Estimated the direction of last night's light...'

 'She found a small brocade carpet spread there. '

'When the owner looked away, greeted other guest, '

'She quietly kicked the corner of the carpet with her foot, '

'Discovered a valve under the carpet.'

'So she came to me quickly, '

'Tell me that she suspected that the"red jade talisman" was hidden
under the valve. '

'I suggested letting me steal it for her. '

'I am an agile ninja. '

'This would have higher success rate! '

He showed a firm, uncompromising look.

'I have heard that the ninja has the ability...'

'Climbs wall and leaps onto roofs. '

Yang Ru eyes glowed.

'Can only hear but not see. '

He smiled regretfully.

'One mid night'

'I came to "Hui qui"appliance shop. '

'Leaped in it though the window, '

'Removed the carpet, '

'Opened the valve with the tools.'

'Then, '

'What I saw was a broken lamp, not the "red jade talisman"...'

'However, I didn't give up, '

'I looked through the broken lamp specifically, '

'Eventually...'

'I took off a shining, red object from the place where is put the
bulb in this lamp. 'The object was just the "red jade talisman" that
she looked forward to getting. '

'At this moment, '

'The owner suddenly broke into, '

'Maybe he already suspected her. '

'Therefore, '

'He went back the shop to inspect in mid night. '

Yamada patted his forehead, said a little hard.

'You killed him! '

Yang Ru' s voice trembled.

'Ninjas do whatever they can do to achieve their goals. '

Yamada closed his eyes, said with some guilty.

Then, he makes a' click', cuts the crab leg on the saucer murderously.

'This was the only way I thought she could safely keep "red jade talisman" and completed her grandfather's wish. '

His face was affectionate.

Yang Ru just keeps silence.

'I didn't expect to drop an insignificant luggage tag, '

'But brought you here.' Yamada said.

Yang Ru doesn' t answer, only drinks a sip of sake.

'As for Miyazaki, '

'He and I were original neighbors and are descendants of the ninja similarly. '

'There were also some friendships with each other. '

'Someday, '

'I had been on phone with her. '

'Forgot to close the door, '

'Let him walk in himself. '

'Heard the conversation between us.'

'Knew that I killed some one.'

'Extorted 100 millon yen from me.'

There was a bit of bitterness in his eyes.

'Blackmail...'

'Today requires 100 millon, tomorrow requires 200 millon...'

'Endlessly!'

He sighed.

'The main thing was that I wanted to protect her. '

'Didn't let Miyazaki hurt her. '

Yamada stubbornly expressed.

'I invited Miyazaki to take the "gold star train", '

'Relaxed completely.'

'Let me and him calm down with each other. '

'Re—negotiated the amount of money.'

'Later, '

'What kind of end was he, you know. '

After listening to Yamada's narrative,

Yang Ru bows his head and meditates for a while.

'I tell you the truth...'

Yang Ru said to Yamada.

'One of the"Seven elites in Tao faction"—Yang Jingsong is my great grandfather. '

'He hoped that late generation would find the"red jade

talisman"and hand it to a person with ability and morality. '

'Play its positive function and benefits humanity. '

'And you killed two people, '

'But only let her take the jade as a private object. '

He looked at Yamada reproachfully.

'Yang Jingsong was a person who achieved his ambition. '

'Was of an even temper.'

'The whole person would become fraternal and generous. '

'He Lei was being despised and hurt. '

'If his family could own this thing, '

'Even if he left world, '

'He could highlight his own value and seek spiritual compensation. '

'It's not really a fault. '

'And I only wanted to be loyal to my love! '

　Yamada said resolutely.

There are footsteps that sound from out side the door.

The door is opened,

Two burly men appear in front of them.

'The female bar boss kaneko once said: '

'"You shall pay what you have done. ". '

'At this time, '

'I just have to pay the price. '

'I guessed when you would come here, '

'And the time we take for talking. '

'Called the police station...'

'At nine o clock, '

'Send some one to take me away in this 'Sakura Dance' room of Moon Kiosk. ' Yamada said it in a dull manner.

Yang Ru was just completely surprised by this sudden scene!

'I would like to sit in this room before accepting sanction. '

'Recalling the time when I was with her here. '

Yamada caresses the hair pin again .

'Now...'

'you had learned the truth of the entire murder case of "Hui qui "appliance shop. '

'It's been a worthwhile trip. '

Yamada glances at Yang Ru deeply.

Then, he collects the hair pin carefully.

Stands up, walks to the two police officers.

'Mr. Yamada...'

'You will never tell me who she is, right? '

Yang Ru stared at the empty porcelain cup in front of him and asked the last question.

Yamada is planning to leave with the police officers...

He just smiles and says:

'Good night, Mr. Yang! '

The side of Hakata Canal...

There are several stalls scattered.

The red lanterns in front of them shine brightly.

Yang Ru is pacing without purpose.

His inter mood is choppy.

Just now...

He heard and saw from Yamada in 'Sakura Dance' room.

He may admire his courage to be loyal to love.

Appreciates his daring to bear the crime.

And in the corner of his heart ...

He has the feeling of idol disillusionment.

The ceramic businessman who has excellent image is real murderer of two murders!

Yang Ru is walking...

The red light in the distance makes him a little dizzy.

Red light, which reminds him of the 'red jade talisman'.

At present,

The 'red jade talisman' is in the hands of a woman.

Spending a night...

Her name is still 'she'.

Yang Ru stopped.

Thinks back carefully.

Yamada held a hairpin in his hand and seemed to very cherish it.

The hairpin should be the woman's item.

Yang Ru quickly takes out the pen and drew the look of the hairpin on the palm.

The hairpin is a branch of pink plum blossoms .

This woman is a Taiwanese.

She must be in Taiwan now.

Otherwise, Yamada won't see the thing, think of the person.

Yang Ru intends to return to Taiwan to find the original owner of the hairpin.

May be he can know the whereabouts of the 'red jade talisman'.

Japan train journey ends!

Another difficulty road of tracing is coming soon!

Yang Ru looks at the front...

Straightens his back and is ready!

Part three
The pains and sorrows of plum blossom hair pin

Yuantong street is a street selling old things.

Sewing cheongsam, selling antique furniture, making ancient cakes...

Here is a hairpin shop called 'Miua Zi'.

Since Yang Ru told Gu chang zch everything about Yamada,

They have become regular customers in this shop.

Yuan Jiging, the boss of 'Miua Zi'.

He builds the hairpins as life mission.

In his mind...

No matter how many years passed,

Only cheongsam and hairpin can show truly feminine style of a woman.

Although the hairpin is already non—trend.

There are not many customers in 'Miua Zi'...

Only some: nostalgic persons, property master of movies and foreign tourists buying souvenirs.

Yuan Jiging doesn't make much money.

However, he is just very satisfied with the fact that his craft can win people's hearts!

And never has a plan to go out of business.

Yang Ru plays his cross—dressing show again.

His reason is that is more convenient for a woman to come to this

shop to explore the news.

Gu chang zch is acting with him.

From time to time,

Yang Ru askes Yuan Jiging about the knowledge of the hairpins.

Yuan Jiging is extremely interested in talking to him.

He thinks that Yang Ru is his bosom friend.

After the conversation,

Yang Ru just buys some hairpins in 'Miua Zi'.

Half moon type, chrysanthemum—like, dragon and phoenix

pattern...various styles.

Yang Ru' s residence gathers a lot of hairpins soon.

Gu chang zch can't help but blame him:

'You wasted too much money. '

'How could it be? '

'Give theses hairpins to the elders as gifts. '

'This will make them feel on top of the world !'

Yang Ru replied this way.

Finally...

Yang Ru bought all kInds of the hairpins in this shop.

But there is no trace of the plum blossom hair pin.

In addition,

He plays a bit tried of his disguised game.

Then, he replies to the original identity.

Goes with Gu chang zch to 'Miua Zi' hair pin shop.

Holds the pattern of plum blossom hair pin, asking Yuan Jiging

Yuan Jiging is not surprised to see' him', just says:

'You were very tricky! '

Yuan Jiging carefully watches the pattern of plum blossom hair pin.

'Each plum blossom has different shape. '

'But is life—like!'

'Especially, '

'The plum blossom branch is fresh and stiff. '

'The whole hair pin is like a new spray of plum blossoms that is just picked off! '

He sincerely praised.

'The man who made this hair pin is a top expert! '

'This kind of craft is not in my shop! '

Yuan Jiging modestly stated.

'You are my familiar customer. '

'I will try my best to help you inquire about the plum blossom hair pin's news. '

Yuan Jiging said to Yang Ru affectionately.

Yang Ru can't hide disappointment.

He gives the pattern of plum blossom hair pin to Yuan Jiging with some confusion.

Says 'thank you' to this boss of 'Miua Zi'.

Just leaves here with Gu chang zch.

They go out of 'Miua Zi',

Walk down the street.

'I reminded you…'

'Always coming to this shop was wasting time and money. '

'There would be no result. '

Gu chang zch complained to Yang Ru.

'Not really, '

Yang Ru defended.

'Because we often went to this shop, '

'The boss of "Miua Zi" was so sincerely to help us find out the news. '

'It's not reliable. '

Gu chang zch did not agree with it.

'May be you can explore women whose surnames are" He". '

Gu chang zch said with great energy.

'Your thought is too direct. '

Yang Ru shook his head indiffterently.

'Listened to Yamada, '

'The woman had experienced all kinds of life. '

'Has a complex identity. '

'She must have several pseudonyms. '

'And her current surname should not be"He". '

Gu chang zch thinks Yang Ru' s words make sense and he will not continue to say it.

Yang Ru whistles suddenly!

It is a Japanese song: 'Love you to the marrow. '

Gu chang zch guesses Yang Ru should remember Yamada's love before blowing it!

Hearing Yang Ru' s whistle,

Gu chang zch feels that he himself is also very ridiculous!

The plum blossom hair pin is an inanimate object he has never seen before.

He moved from pillar to post for it.

Gets tired physically and mentally.

How long will this day of finding the plum blossom hair pin last?

Someone is sending flyers.

Yang Ru detours, doesn' t want to make garbage.

Gu chang zch just takes a flyer.

He has no intention of glance at it,

Immediately shouted:

'We find it! '

This is a flyer for the stage drama of 'Back light' troupe.

The name of the play is called 'Art sea mystery '!

It is set in the early years of Republic of China.

The shapes of several major characters were printed on the flyer.

Warlord, hooligan holds a cigarette between his lips, old scholastic wearing a suit, foreign missionary...

The most eyes catching is the heroine standing in the middle!

There is a line of text next to it:

'Tao Hong plays the actress Xia Bing Yan'

She wears a red cheongsam with a pink hair pin.

The style and color of the hair pin are exactly the same as they are looking for.

Yang Ru holds the flyer.

His finger is slightly trembling!

He stared at the plum blossom hair pin on the flyer for one minute.

Then, his mind turns quickly!

'I think...' He considered.

'I can ask someone to do something for us. '

Yang Ru found his colleague from past.

Zhu mingqi, who specializes in interviewng drama news.

Asks him to arrange for them to meet Tao Hong.

Part three   The pains and sorrows of plum blossom hair pin

The actress knows to please the press.

She promises it immediately!

Taking advantage of the rest time of 'Art sea mystery' s rehearsal,

Yang Ru and Gu chang zch come to Tao Hong's private lounge.

At this time,

Her hair is messy.

No make up on her face.

Just wears an ordinary blue dress, white shoes have stains.

She looks extremely tired.

Can't see her star style!

Yang Ru and Gu chang zch meet Tao Hong for the first time.

She also has a good attitude and has been smiling.

'Have a seat, please. '

She said.

'No problem with signature. '

'The photo is temporarily not available. '

After the three of them are seated,

Tao Hong was so happy to express.

'Ms. Tao Hong...'

'In fact, '

'We have some thing to ask you. '

Yang Ru said a little embarrassed.

Tao Hong knows that Yang Ru and Gu chang zch are not fans of her own and her attitude is colder.

'What we want to ask is about the plum blossom hair pin. '

Yang Ru said cautiously.

'The plum blossom hair pin? '

'It was a masterpiece of our former head. '

'His name is Luo Kai Chung. '

'He usually loved to make such old thing in addition to managing the troupe. '

There was a kind of contempt in her words.

'But he seemed to only make this plum blossom type. '

'Never saw him doing anything else. '

She added that.

'Later, '

'This hair pin became a symbol of the identity of the heroine of 'Art sea mystery'!   '

'An actress in this role could also have a few private plum blossom hair pins. '

'But this was nothing. '

'Who would bring this old thing out? '

Tao Hong takes out the cigarette and rudely smokes it.

'So, do you know Mr. Yamada Hikaru? '

Yang Ru continued to ask.

'Yamada Hikaru? '

'What's that? '

'Oh, it 's Janpanese name! '

She got it.

'I don't know this person at all. '

She waved her hand impatiently.

'But his lover also has a such plum blossom hair pin. '

Yang Ru said.

'As you said, '

'Yamada's lover is that bitch——Luo Xueyen. '

'Bitch?'

Yang Ru and Gu chang zch were stunned by this vulgar noun.

'Wasn't she? '

Tao Hong's voice became very sharp.

'Think that year, '

'Regardless of appearance, acting, reputation...'

'I am all better than her. '

'But she played the super character—— Xia BingYan. '

'Why? '

'Just because she is Luo Kai Chung's lover. '

'So no matter how hard I tried, '

'I couldn' t win this role. '

She is more and more passionate and anger is constantly rising.

'But when Luo Kai Chung retired, '

'She lost dependence. '

'"Art sea mystery" s heroine is me after all. '

She smokes proudly.

'Later, '

'I heard that she arrived in Japan. '

'Actually became a servant! '

Tao Hong has some gloating and her mood seems to have calmed down.

'Yamada should be the man she met in Japan. '

She quenched the smoke and said.

'Do you have Luo Xueyen's photograph? '

Yang Ru asked Tao Hong.

'How can I have photo of my enemy? '

'Just have it, '

'But also tear it apart. '

'You want to know about Luo Xueyen...'

'Just ask Luo Kai Chung. '

She takes a piece of cosmetic paper from the dressing table.

'This is Luo Kai Chung's address and phone number. '

She wrote a few words and numbers on cosmetic paper and gave it to Yang Ru.

'Appreciate it! '

Yang Ru took the small piece of paper and thanked her.

'Ms. Tao...'

'Sorry to bother you so long time. '

Part three   The pains and sorrows of plum blossom hair pin

'We should leave now. '
Yang Ru and Gu chang zch stood up at the same time.
'Please. '
Tao Hong lowered her eyelids, said.

So, Yang Ru and Gu chang zch quickly leave the simple and crude
room.
They all feels a serious sense of loss from the middle—aged
actress!

In Luo Kai Chung's private study...
He entertains Yang Ru and Gu chang zch with enthusiasm.
'I have not been in contact with young people for a long time. '
Luo Kai Chung lamented.
'I meet you today. '
'I am full of energy. '
He stretches his arms to improve it.
'You are too kind! '
'We are bothering you too much. '
Yang Ru responded politely.
'How come...'
'As as long as you don' t get impatience with old man' s words. '
Luo Kai Chung expressed warmly and funnily.

Both of them just smiles at the old head of 'Back light' troupe and shake their heads.

'My grand father once opened a theater in Shanghai. '

'And my farther founded the "Back light" troupe. '

'Fortunately, '

'I don't reject the drama. '

'So I inherited it. '

Luo Kai Chung said with positive tone.

'I found Luo Xueyen from outside. '

'She is an average—looking girl. '

'Had not received orthodox acting training.'

'But I can saw that she had extraordinary potential! '

'She could master a character very quickly. '

'And injected the role with new ideas.'

'Tightly attracted the attentions of the audience.'

'The whole stage would be vivid and bright for her! '

Luo Kai Chung did not hide his extreme appreciation and love for her.

'After she entered the troupe, '

'She performed a play "The cataclysm of ice and snow". '

'Its story was...'

'A white wild goose changed a woman, '

'Was injured in th snow.'

'Then, she was rescued by a young hunter. '

'Furthermore, '

'They had been getting married. '

'But after all, '

'People and elves were different. '

'They were finally separated. '

Luo Kai Chung continued to tell.

'It sounds like a sad and graceful love story. '

Gu chang zch commented on the side.

'How to describe Luo Xueyen's performance? '

Luo Kai Chung leaned his head and considered.

'She could simultaneously make a gesture of coexistence between human—being and wild goose, '

'Was just like a real wild goose elf! '

'Made every one be stunned!'

'Her stage name" Luo Xueyen" was just from this play. '

'When the play was over, '

'I and she became lovers. '

'Our love was naturally not optimistic. '

'My wife had just passed away, '

'And my age is much elder than her. '

'Every one criticized this love. '

'Although we were really in love.'

He showed his sorrow.

'She served as the"Art sea mystery"'s heroine...'

'This incident caused the hatred of other actresses. '

'They said that she was a prostitute, seeking glory in selling her body. ’

‘I explained it many times to everyone: ’

‘"Business is business, friends are friends. ". ’

‘Because only Luo Xueyen’s acting skill could express the complexity of this role"Xia BingYan"! ’

‘I just chose her to take this role. ’

His facial expression looks very serious.

‘I understand your consistent loyalty to drama. ’

Yang Run sincerely supported Luo Kai Chung.

‘Something was interesting...’

‘I like to make some small items like hair—pins at my usual time. ’

‘ Luo Xueyen put on the plum blossom hair pin I made and stepped on to stage. ’

‘This made her become noble and charming in this play! ’

‘Since then, ’

‘The plum blossom hair pin had become a symbol of" Xia Bing Yan". ’

‘And was also Luo Xueyen’s love! ’

‘Of course, she owned a few plum blossom hair pins privately. ’

Facing this past,

Luo Kai Chung is full of warmth and thoughts.

‘Her other lover Yamada Hikaru also regards it as a love thing. ’

Yang Run thought but could not say.

'Our romance could not continue...'

'Except for the eyes of people, '

'Another reason was my son. '

'He didn't want me to marry again. '

'And he had to face a such young step mother. '

'You obeyed him? '

Gu chang zch didn't take it for granted.

'He is my only son. '

Luo Kai Chung regretted to admit it.

'After our love was over, '

'My physical condition was not good also. '

'Then, '

'I transferred the troupe to others. '

'At about the same time, '

'Luo Xueyen also left the troupe. '

There are tears in Luo Kai Chung's eyes.

'After a time, '

'I heard that she went to Japan to a family to assistant housework. '

'May be this was the actual job she want to do most. '

'Instead of living on an illusory stage.'

Luo Kai Chung seems to be relived about such Luo Xue yen.

'In recent years, '

'It was said that she returned to Taiwan again. '

'I didn't ask anymore, '

'Because I had long been unrelated to her.'

He accepted the fate.

'Do you keep any items of Luo Xueyen? '

Gu chang zch asked Luo Kai Chung earlier than Yang Ru.

'I am so sorry. '

'After we broke up, '

'My son ruined my all collections about her. '

'Video tapes, clippings, photos...'

'How was your son again?

Gu chang zch cried extremely dissatisfied .

He can't undstand...

A troupe leader who had rich life experience.

Why should he keep obeying a junior?

'He was violent. '

'But it also made me not see the things, not think of her. '

Luo Kai Chung's mood was calm.

'It is not difficulty to know Luo Xueyen's appearance.

'Her past fans should have her photos. '

Luo Kai Chung said to them.

Gu chang zch and Yang Ru thanks Luo Kai Chung and left.

For this moment,

Gu chang zch feels that a sense of decadence is creeping into Yang Ru' s eyes.

So he encourages him to grab his right shoulder and shakes it a few times!

Gu chang zch and Yang Ru go together to watch the stage play 'Art sea mystery' in the afternoon.

Gu chang zch admires the drama wholeheartly.

Yang Ru is barely watching it.

He looks at his nails to think about things for a while.

All of a sudden,

He looks around to observe the reactions of audience.

Before watching the drama,

Gu chang zch and Yang Ru reaches a consensus:

They come here to explore the news of Luo Xueyen.

Do not need to pay much attentions to the plots of the play.

Two young men are used to modern movies with fast paces and Acousto— optic powers.

And don't quite accept the stage play.

Tao Hong works hard to perform the role 'Xia BingYan'.

At the beginning,

  Xia BingYan is a a shining movie star!

Then, she becomes a smart and capable intelligence agent!

Finally,

she turns into a woman who struggle with love and pain.

She recalls:

Originally,

She was a native country girl.

Made a living with her dreams to the city.

But she suffered with bulling.

After entering the entertainment circle,

She also helped people to find information.

Just didn't expect to be hostile to the man she loved.

From time to time,

She has to sway between tasks and personal feelings.

Nothing to do with pain!

The ending of this play is...

She only lets go of it and leave.

'The plots were not bad, '

'But the whole stage looked a bit messy. '

When the play was over, Gu chang zch couldn't wait to express his opinion.

After the play,

There are many people waiting at the elevator door!

Yang Ru proposes to take the stairs and it will be faster.

So they walk up to stairs together.

'I almost fell asleep while watching the play. '

Yang Run yawned, talked while walking.

'But we also knew the storyline of 'Art sea mystery'. '

Gu chang zch still retained the interesting after play and said.

'The drama expressed a variety of feelings and emotions between people. '

'These complex feelings and emotions formed a huge net! '

Gu chang zch made a circle in the air.

'And people were struggling in this net. '

'Couldn't get out of it.'

He spread his hands and showed helplessness.

'So, you are very touched by this play! '

Yang Ru grinned at Gu chang zch.

They come to the stairs.

See the aged with a cane.

And his paces are awkward.

Yang Ru and Gu chang zch help him down stairs together.

'How is it good!'

'Suddenly, '

'There are two more sons! '

  The aged's face expanded a smile.

'Why are your children not accompanying you? '

Gu chang zch couldn't help but ask the aged.

'They refused to accompany me and blamed me...'

'Why do I go to see the such old drama? '

'It's a waste of life. '

The aged felt sentimental about his children's attitudes.

'If you like, '

'We can send you home. '

After finishing the last stage,

Yang Run comforted the aged like this.

'But I want to ask you drink tea first. '

The aged said kindly.

'Helping you go down stairs just a trifle. '

'You really don't need to pay for it. '

Gu chang zch hurriedly shook his hand and refused.

'It's not like that, '

The aged retorted gently.

'You made me feel surprise! '

'At your age, '

'You should only pay attention to the latest video game and mobile phone. '

'Why did you come to watch the old— style stage play? '

'So I am very interested to talk to you both! '

The aged looked at them with a smile.

'Or are you not willing to be with an old man? '

Said by the aged.

Yang Ru and Gu chang zch can no longer refuse.

The'Reed Cottage'is a historic tea house.

There is nothing to decorate it.

Even the furnishings are not neat.

But it has all kinds of tea.

Jin Xuan, Wen Moutain, Ali Moutain, oolong, Longquon....

In addition,

The 'Reed Cottage' also offers some snacks to guests.

Snow flakes, pine nut cakes, cookies...

A few regular customers just habitually order the cheapest black tea.

Smoked the cigarettes, put their feet up...

Listen to the radio, read the news papers...

Just spend a long time in this store.

The 'Reed Cottage' always care nothing of it.

The old neighbors are just like their family.

This is the unique human touch of the tea house.

Yang Ru and Gu chang zch can see that the aged is very familiar with the tea house.

The aged greets them to sit down.

He ordered three cups of longjing tea and some snacks；mashed date cakes, almond strips, candied fruits…

The aged says his name is Zong Weimin.

He had retired from post office, is currently idle at home.

After Zong Weimin asked their names，

He starts a conversation.

'The actress who played Xia Bing Yan was qualified.'

'But still some one was better than her.'

He was outspoken.

'Her name was Luo…'

Zong Weimin could not remember her full name at the moment.

'Luo Xueyen!'

Yang Ru and Gu chang zch said next.

'Yeah…'

'You actually know!'

His face registered surprise.

'Yes! It is Luo Xueyen!'

'A character wants to impress audience……'

'And make them be unforgettable...'

'The actor or actress who performs must give them a sense of soul resonance. '

'Not just a simple appreciation of a character. '

'There are very few actors who can reach this realm. '

'Luo Xueyen is one of them! '

Zong Weimin discussed his drama concept.

'Are you her fan? '

Gu chang zch asked him.

'I am not her fan...'

'Just appreciate her! '

Zong Weimin was a little embarrassed.

'Does uncle Zong have Luo Xueyen's image record? '

Yang Ru took the opportunity to explore.

'You are helping your elders inquire about her news...'

'So you came to see this play, right? '

Zong Weimin thought it was reasonable to speculate.

Yang Ru and Gu chang zch don't deny it.

'I don't have. '

'But I can look for it from some of my friends. '

Zong Weimin said.

'Thank you, uncle Zong...'

'We really appreciate your help. '

Yang Ru gives Zong Weimin a thankful gesture.

After talking about the play,

Zong Weimin begins to recount his past as the ordinary old man.

Thinks about the wife who passed away.

Tells the glory of his past.

Yang Ru andGu chang zch all cooperate with listening.

They quite understand:

You are willing to have patient to have a chat with a lone old man,

this is the thing that makes him be happy the most.

So Zong Weimin spends a warm time in the tea house like that.

Leaving the 'Reed Cottage',

Zong Weimin says that he don't want to go home early.

They also accompany him around.

The sky is all black.

The lights are scattered.

  Two young man are holding the old man intimately.

This movement makes Zong Weimin constantly claiming that he is

so happy today!

There are several galleries and art shops on the street side.

At this time,

The appearances of these stores are not clear.

And Zong Weimin is very interested in browing each store.

He stops at a painting shop called 'Yi Xing'

The light in this store is much brighter than in others.

'We meet her!'

Zong Weimin stared at the painting in the window and said.

'Who?'

Yang Ru asked.

'Luo Xueyen!'

Yang Ru and Gu chang zch follow Zong Weimin's sight.

L ook at the woman in the painting.

She has a sharp chin, think eyebrows and slightly melancholy eyes.

Reveals a wisdom after the vicissitudes of life. Zong Weimin moved

and gazes at her almost reverently.

Yang Ru watches the woman in the painting, thinks:

'Where can I find her?'

Gu chang zch just turns his eyes away.

Has been thinking for a while.

Vaguely...

He seems to smell a scent of bread cream that swirls from the air.

Friday evening,

 It is time for office workers to meet weekend.

On the occasion of the traffic spike,

It is also the climax of the 'Jubilance'bakery's business！

Customers are crowded here to buy things.

For the general public,

Bread is still the most affordable food and can bring satiety.

Jiang Yihui is so busy.

She accounts, fills breads and greets guests.

Although there is air conditioning,

The sweat is still falling from her forehead.

She has to constantly wipe the sweat and tries to maintain her grace and smile.

Yang Ru and Gu chang zch open the door and come in.

Gu chang zch go to Jiang Yihui by himself.

Yang Ru is standing alone for time being.

There is a girl likes a clerk has been smirking at Yang Ru.

Yang Ru feels inexplicable,

But also politely nods to her.

'Today...'

'I am not visiting the boss of 'Jubilance' bakery—Jiang Yihui. '

'But the genius actress— Luo Xueyen.'

'The lover of Mr. Yamada.'

'Perhaps she can also be called the owner of "red jade talisman" at the present time！ '

Gu chang zch approached Jiang Yihui and said.

Jiang Yihui rubs her apron with her hands, then, says mockingly:

'You must have experienced a lot of setbacks to find me. '

'Can't wait to talk with me, right? '

'But you know the current situation...'

She looked around the crowd in the store.

'Wait two more days and then talk about it. '

Jiang Yihui proposed.

Gu chang zch no longer enforces her.

'The time is wrong...'

'We must make second visit. '

Gu chang zch went to Yang Ru and said.

Just as they are turning and preparing to leave 'Jubilance' bakery,

But there is a voice coming from behind them.

'Elder brother Ru!'

Yang Ru turns around,

He finds that it was from the girl who just smirked at him.

'I am Xiao meng. '

'Your neighbor——Xiao meng!'

The girl took Yang Ru, yelled and jumped

'I always smiled at you. '

'But You had no reaction. '

Yang Ru examines the girl in front of him.

Round face, big eyes, flat nose...

Still has the shadow of crying girl when he was a youngster.

'You grow up and became so beautiful. '

'Don't say it is me, '

'Many people will not recognize you. '

Yang Ru dealt politely.

'You finally remembered it, elder brother Ru! '

Xiao meng screamed joyfully.

Then, she talks about the childhood with her elder brother Ru...

A boy whose nick name was 'gecko' often bullied her.

Alder brother Ru just helped her to fight back him.

Alder brother Ru was not only her patron saint, but also her best companion.

He took her to rent comic books, to catch shrimps and butterflies.

She was in a bad mood...

Alder brother Ru bought her popsicles and hot dogs.

She was bored...

He imitated cartoon characters and played with her.

Xiao meng is completely immersed in her childhood!

Yang Ru introduces Gu chang zch to her, Stresses that he is a regular customer in 'Jubilance' bakery.

She only hurriedly greets.

Just can't wait to return to topic.

'My childhood was equal to the name "elder brother Ru"! '

Xiao meng is full of admiration for Yang Ru.

In fact,

Yang Ru has been barely listening.

After all, he never thought about Xiao meng for years.

His past events with her have never been placed in his heart.

And Xiao meng is holding on this past.

'I lost contact with you after you moved. '

'I was sad for a long time. '

She regretted to tell Yang Ru.

'Fortunately, '

'God has eyes. '

'I and you met again! '

Xiao meng replied with a pleasant tone.

'I am currently working in this store. '

'You can come to see me at any time. '

'It is very convenient. 'Xiao meng said to Yang Ru briskly.

'Yes, Yes...'

Yang Ru said in a row, but his look was not comfortable.

Gu chang zch watches the scene, can't help but secretly laughs.

'Not bad, brat...'

'You can write an article "My romantic history in bakery"! '

They just got out of bakery, Gu chang zch made fun of Yang Ru.

'What's romantic history? '

'She was just a witless young girl then. '

Yang Ru displeased refuted.

'That should be the childhood sweetheart. '

Gu chang zch was naughty, continued to tease him.

Yang Ru no longer responds to Gu chang zch.

He is glued to the high—hanging golden signboard 'Jubilance'.

Happy gold—like wheat shimmers under sun.

Wheat is the row source of the flour of bread.

He also realizes that 'Jubilance' bakery has a special bright and warm style!

But he is a little sensitive:

The boss of 'Jubilance' bakery— Luo Xueyen had a latent sense of loss on her nonstop smiles.

'Hope she doesn't have any problem. '

Yang Ru prayed silently.

This is a carefree and contented night.

Moon light is clear   .

The shadows of flowers flicker on balcony.

The temperature is not too cold or too hot, just right.

Anyone feels comfortable at this moment.

Jiang Yihui wears an orange robe.

Brings a cup of tea, sitting on a wicker chair of balcony leisurely.

Summer is over, entering the autumn.

However, the weather in Taiwan is very weird.

It is still hot during the day,

But it gets cool at night.

Autumn is Yamada's favorite season!

He enjoys the colors of autumn foliage.

Prefers the autumn's leisure.

Yamada is not only her lover, but also her enternal soul mate!

Whether they are together or not,

Their spirits are connected forever!

She met him for the first time at his home.

He was arrogant, bossy and impolite.

But she could see he was also brilliant and kind!

Late,

She was determined to take care of his terrible disease.

Of course!

She did not want to return his favor.

Others were hard to believe,

She was so affectionate to guard a man!

Recalling the past...

Various emotions linger her inside.

Jiang Yihui takes a sip of tea and smoothes her emotions.

She stares at the pattern on the cup ： a flying wild geese!

This reminds her of her drama career...

'Stag play sprite! '

People always like to call her like this.

Yes!

Luo Xueyen!

An actress who brought countless laughter, tears and touch to audiences!

Today,

It is not many people who remember her.

Although she regrets,

She can still accept it .

Luo Kai Chung made her!

Let an ordinary girl shone on the stage!

She and he are no longer lovers,

She still appreciates him.

Jiang Yihui whirls the cup and recalls this romance...

She and Luo Kai Chung's love is unforgettable.

Her love with Yamada is the input of whole soul!

There is osmanthus flavor floating from the inside.

The osmanthus cake is ready!

Jiang Yihui lays down the cup and goes into kitchen.

Turns off the fire,

Dishes the osmanthus cake in the steamer into the plate.

Holding this osmanthus cake,

She returns to the balcony.

Puts the osmanthus cake on the end table in front of her.

The osmanthus cake is soft and dense.

Gives off an enticing smell!

Yamada dosen't like the scent of flowers,

But loves osmanthus flavor.

Excludes the sweets,

Just is full of praise for the osmanthus cake she makes.

At first,

She did pay a lot for Yamada.

Later,

He made a greater sacrifice for her.

Killed, stole...

It was all for 'red jade talisman'!

However, his sacrifice was extremely valuable!

She now has a complete grasp of this treasure of Tao world!

Jiang Yihui looks up the night sky.

She seems to hear the call of her grandfather——He Lei from this

deep, black curtain.

He left the message to the descendants of future generations:

He was most despised in 'Seven elites in Tao faction'.

'A silly clown, there would be no achievement. '

Everyone looked at him like that.

He didn't act, but his descendants would have.

He encouraged them to get 'red jade talisman' at any cost!

Brought the honor to the family.

Mastered the power of the Tao world!

His grand daughter—— He Yi completed his instruct!

He Yi is her real name.

She had become a prostitute, called to be Aili.

It is similar to the pronunciation of Taiwanese 'love you'.

Entering the troupe...

Luo Kai Chung gave her a stage name—Luo Xueyen.

Went to Yamada's home help with housework,

She had another Japanese name—Akiko.

Back to Taiwan...

She opened the bakery.

Her name is' Jiang Yihui'.

Sells the general food.

Turns back into a thoroughly ordinary person!

Her life began with being despised, just like her grandfather—He Lei.

She lived hard and bitterly.

At this moment,

She recalls all her past.

Just feels that her life was so splendid!

The wind becomes bigger.

Lifts off the white floor curtain.

The blurred clouds in the night sky seems to flutter gently.

'Is time up? '

Jiang Yihui asked herself.

She walks into the bed room,

Takes off her orange robe and puts on a peach color cheongsam
with white edge.

Wears her hair up and fixes it with clips.

Then, Plugs in the plum blossom hair pin.

Faintly layers makeup.

Takes a mirror to look at herself.

Finally...

She dresses up as Xia Bing Yan in 'Art sea mystery'!

She used to dress like this in front of Yamada.

It amazed him!

This may be just the freshness of the Japanese looking at Chinese clothing.

She should not be so gorgeous.

Yamada also had greatest esteem for the plum blossom hair pin.

Said its technology was impeccable!

Yamada carries the plum blossom hair pin, like guarding her soul.

'The plum blossom hair pin is attached not only to her own love, but also to more complex grievances: Luo Kai Chung's son hatred her, the actresses were jealous of her in troup...'

She takes off the hair pin and looks at it with heavy thoughts and then puts it on again.

Suddenly,

Jiang Yihui remembers something she should do.

She opens the drawer and takes off the letter papper and envelope.

Hurries to write a few lines of words of the letter papper.

After writing...

She seals it into the envelope.

Writes the name of the recipient on it.

Then,

Leaves the letter on the dressing table.

Jiang Yihui picks up the osmanthus cake.

Eats it bit by bit.

'One hundred percent delicious food!'

She scored herself.It is really strange!

This was the most successful one she made it 。

She seems to see Yamada's happy and satisfied look when he ate

the osmanthus cake.

This is not an illusion.

It should be that Yamada is coming to take her away.

One week ago,

Jiang Yihui got the news...

Yamada committed suicide in prison.

No one knows him better than her.

In order to defend a dignity belonging to the ninja,

He was voluntarily arrested to express responsibility.

And he didn't want others to execute himself, chose to self—

destruct!

Tetrodotoxin was placed in the osmanthus cake.

At present,

The toxin has already occurred!

Jiang Yihui begins to be limb paralysis, dizziness and has an excruciating pain in belly.

Yamada waves to her not far away...

Jiang Yihui shows a smile on her lips:

They can be together forever finally!

The pain disappears.

Jiang Yihui feels that her soul is out of body...

Flies lightly to the love!

Part four

The treasures were left in the world

Half a month after Jiang Yihui's funeral…

Yang Ru, Xiao meng and Gu chang zch are sitting around a small round table.

A tabulae is on the table.

It says:

'Xiao meng:

There are three invaluable treasures in my life.

One of them is Mr. Yamada…

Now, I have been with him,

And can keep the treasure forever.

As for the other two treasures,

I don't care about any of their results.

Whether they are permanently hidden or instantly discovered.

You are not my birth daughter…

However, we are in love with real mother and daughter.

I am unmarried.

But I have you——a such lovely daughter.

This is a blessing!

The bakery is handed over to you for management.

The house and the limited money are also left to you.

I have already clearly explained these in my will.

Believe that you will live very well!

Yihui's last words. '

'She was very generous to you. '

When Yang Ru and Gu chang zch finished reading the tabulae, said

to Xiao meng at the same time.

'Aunt Yihui said that I was her blessing. '

'In fact, '

'She was just my savior! '

Xiao meng shook her head with choking voice.

'You know, elder brother Ru, '

She turned to Yan Ru.

'My family was bad. '

'A drunk father liked to gamble and be on drink. '

'My mother left home early and abandoned us. '

'I had never lived a warm family life for a day. '

Her tears dripped down.

'I almost went to work at erotic place for father's gambling debt. '

'Fortunately, '

'I had the distant relative——aunt Yihui. '

'She helped us pay off debt. '

'Let me work in the bakery. '

'Included full board and lodging.'

'I asked her to deduct my salary to pay her back. '

'But she never did that. '

'Even didn't mention anything to pay our debt. '

Xiao meng said appreciatively.

'Yes...'

'I treated aunt Yihui as biological mother. '

'But I never expected that she left everything to me. '

She sobbed gently.

Yang Ru touches her head and expresses comfort.

Gu chang zch just hands her a piece of facial tissue.

'I am so sorry, Xiao meng...'

'You had to see aunt Yihui's tabulae again for us, '

'And let you be sad one more time. '

Yang Ru felt remorse.

'Don't say that, elder brother Ru...'

'I should do anything for you. '

Xiao meng wiped her tears with facial tissue, said insistently.

'May I ask you a question? '

Yang Ru saw her emotions have been slightly calm, so asked.

'Sure. '

Xiao meng nodded.

'The other two treasures aunt Yihui mentioned in her tabulae. '

'One of them should be" red jade talisman". '

'Do you know what the other treasure, Xiao meng? '

His face was full of doubts.

'I am sorry, elder brother Ru...'

'I don't know. '

'Although aunt Yihui quite took care of me, '

'She didn't reveal her private secrets to me. '

'I also had never known the relationship between her and Mr. Yamada.'

Xiao meng clearly and surely expressed.

'I guess this way...'

Yang Ru bitted his lips, thought.

'If we can find another treasure, '

'Can use it as a clue to get" red jade talisman". '

'But now it seems that there is no way to do this. '

Yang Ru looks a bit annoyed.

'Will not, elder brother Ru. '

'I'll do my best to help you. '

'You can definitely find " red jade talisman"!   '

Xiao meng grabbed Yang Ru's arm and screamed eagerly.

'Trouble you. '

Yang Ru didn't respond very strongly.

Gu chang zch can see:

Yang Ru has regretted his cold attitude toward this ' childhood sweetheart' in the bakery.

At this time,

It is at dusk.

Yang Ru is looking at the sky through the window.

A big piece of burning red sun set clouds in it.

He ponders:

'This is a sight of typhoon! '

'The refrigerator is empty. '

'In the night, '

'The wind and rain will come. '

'I need to go out and buy something right away. '

'If I stay a little longer, '

'I am afraid I will be not able to leave. '

Yang Ru walks to the door…

But the door rings!

Opens the door,

Gu chang zch brings a sack of foods to come in.

Then…

He takes out every kinds of foods from the sack.

Instant noodle, canned tuna, pork floss, breads, fruits, ring pull

cans of soda and coke.

'The storm has not yet come…'

'My love is first. '

'Give the typhoon's supplies to my young master. '

Gu chang zch raised his eye brows at Yang Ru, said.

'You don't have to accompany your real master? '

Yang Ru opens a can of coke and drinks himself.

'You mean uncle lin? '

'He is quite strong!   '

'Do you see me as a weak animal? '

Yang Ru asked Gu chang zch.

'Also spent a period of time, '

'We still do not find the trace of" red jade talisman". '

'Uncle lin is as calm as ever. '

'You always look downhearted. '

Facing Yang Ru' s depressive attitude,

Gu chang zch can not help but feel sympathy.

'Who said that we must not find it? '

Yang Ru swigged back the coke, showed the determination not to
give up.

'Do you have any news from your lover? '

Gu chang zch still didn't forget to mock Yang Ru.

'How many times do I need to tell you? '

'Xiao meng—she—is—not—my—lover.'

Yang Ru ground his teeth in anger.

He is extremely dissatisfied with Gu chang zch.

But his ear roots are inexplicably feverish!

'Tell the truth…'

Gu chang zch was no longer joking, really talking about things.

'Now, '

'Jiang Yihui's house belongs to Xiao meng. '

'If we ask her, '

'Let's thoroughly search the house once. '

'Maybe we can find the stuff " red jade talisman"! '

Gu chang zch thinks his words are feasible.

'We don't have to this yet. '

Yang Ru was not keen to respond.

'Besides, '

'Jiang Yihui may not put the" red jade talisman" in her home. '

'It is also possible to hide it far away. '

Yang Ru drains off the coke.

The drink really makes him be more and more bored!

'Temporarily threw away the annoying problem. '

'I am famished. '

Gu chang zch takes out of a loaf of green union bread.

Regardless of the image,

He gobbles up it.

'This bread was what I brought at another store. '

'The green union bread made by 'Jubilance'bakery is still more delicious!'

'Green unions are full of flavor. '

'Bread is softer. '

The food was held in the mouth, Gu chang zch said unclearly.

After eating more than half of the bread,

Gu chang zch puts down it and says:

'I don't know how Xiao meng manages the bakery? '

'She is new hand after all. '

'Jiang Yihui was different. '

'She handled things round and thoughtfully. '

'Also won the championship of the bread competition!'

'Her technique for making bread was really nothing to say. '

'Did she once win the championship of the bread competition? '

When Yang Ru heard it, he quickly asked.

'I had suggested this way...'

'Showing the trophy in the store to attract more customers.'

'She just said that she was completely recognized by consumers for quality. '

' No need to show off. '

'So I won't say more. '

After Gu chang zch finished eating the bread,

He opens a can of grape soda.

Half lies on the sofa...

Leisurely drinks it with a straw.

Yang Ru's eyes are bright!

The whole person is glowing!

'Should the trophy be one of the other two treasures? '

'If we are lucky enough, '

'Maybe you and me can find" red jade talisman" from the trophy! '

The sky is dark all over.

It stars to wind and rain.

And the storm is getting stronger and stronger!

Yang Ru listens to the deafening sound of the wind and rain.

Thinks:

Hopes this typhoon can pass away quickly.

He can go to Xiao meng's residence to find out the trophy and study it.

Only one and half days.

The typhoon passed.

But the scene is disordered outside.

Fallen huge trunks, signboards, dead branches, leaves... scatter everywhere.

Yang Ru just doesn't care all.

He and Gu chang zch rushes Xiao meng's residence—Jiang Yihui's previous home.

As soon as they enter the house,

Yang Ru had already told his purpose to Xiao meng on the phone.

So She immediately takes the trophy from the display cabinet in

the living room and gives it to them.

The trophy is very chic!

It is the shape of a French baguette.

And its design is actually alive and can be opened!

It's no difficulty to open the 'baguette'.

But it is empty, not being put into anything.

The wooden mat under the trophy is also solid.

There is no way to hide anything.

It happens to this time...

Somebody visits Xiao meng.

The visitor is a 70 years old grand mother.

A shock of white hair, humpbacked.

It's not flexible when she walks.

And she is very likely to come from the country, takes a flower

cloth bag.

Xiao meng instantly sees her, just shouts relieved:

'Four grandaunt, '

'You finally come! '

'Aunt Yihui repeatedly emphasized in her will: '

'Be sure to give the two colors, Japanese garden pattern food box to you. '

'She often said when she was alive…'

'As soon as you saw the food box, '

'Always appreciated it for a long time!'

'Praised it again and again!'

'But it was no wonder…

'Aunt Yihui spent a sum of money to order it from the expert who made the food boxes in Japan. '

'It is unique one in the world! '

'And the food box is extremely strong and not easy to damage. '

'If you don't appear today, '

'Then, I will personally visit you and hand it over to you. '

Xiao meng took four grandaunt, muttered.

Who knows that four grandaunt hears Xiao meng's words and actually cries!

'Oh, what's wrong with this? ' '

'Young people died earlier than the elder.'

'He Yi…'

She called Jiang Yihui's real name.

'Her bakery was operated so well! '

'There was also a clever and cute child companion—Xiao meng. '

She looked at Xiao meng.

'She should be very satisfied. '

'Why did she still suffer from suicide? '

'Was it because she didn't have a husband? '

Four grandaunt was sad and resentful.

'Aunt Yihui was an extraordinary woman!'

Xiao meng solemnly declared.

'Had her own specific thinking and acting style! '

'She wanted to choose to leave the world early, '

'Nobody could stop her. '

'You and me are her love ones in the world, '

'We must work hard to live peacefully and happily. '

'Don't let her worry about us in another world. '

Xiao meng wiped four grandaunt's tears, maturely persuaded.

'Introuce you two young talents.'

Xiao men said to four grandaunt briskly.

'Yang Ru, Gu chang zch...'

She made a gesture to each of them separately.

'They are my friends. '

'Gu chang zch was even aunt Yihui's familiar customer. '

'Four grandaunt is the youngest sister of aunt Yihui's dead

mother. '

'Aunt Yihui always said...'

'She's her other mother. '
'I just call her "the fourth grandaunt". '
'We have nice relationship too! '
Xiao meng hugged the fourth grandaunt and said with a smile.
'I am going to make tea. '
'You talk for a while. '

After Xiao meng enters,
They sit on the sofa in the living room and gossip.
'You were He Yi's regular customer. '
'Had you tried every product of her store? '
The fourth grandaunt first asked Gu chang zch.
'Yes! '
'I tasted all kinds of bread in 'Jubilance' bakery. '
'But I liked the green union bread most. '
He answered honestly.
'This salt bread is really delightful!   '
'It also can be the classic of 'Jubilance' bakery. '
The fourth grandaunt smiled with approve.
'But I think...'
'The best snack He Yi made in her whole life. '
'Not the bread and cakes that were sold in bakery, '
'Nor was her winning creation.'
'It— was— the—osmanthus—cake!'

She said word by word, voice was full of power.

'She only made the special products for her dearest persons. '

'Not for sale. '

'This was may be a way for her to express her feelings. '

When the fourth grandaunt talked about the word 'feelings', she whimpered again .

'The cake is originally a normal snack...'

'He Yi just made it soft and fragrant. '

'And turned it into the shape of a boat. '

'Like a court dessert! '

Referring to her niece's masterpiece, the fourth grandaunt's face lightened.

'I used to ask for recipe of osmanthus cake. '

'She just answered me: '

'"I am sorry. "'

'"The recipe is my private collection. ". '

'Then, she said:

'"Maybe someday is coming...". '

 '"It belongs to you! ". '

'But I didn't expect it...'

' "Someday" was when she died. '

'If I had known this, '

'I would rather not get that recipe for a life time. '

The fourth grandaunt talked and felt sad again.

Xiao meng comes over holding a tray with tea set.

After she put a cup of tea in front of everyone,

Yang Ru suddenly stands up and says:

'Xiao meng...'

'Did aunt Yihui leave anything related to the recipe? '

'If there is...'

'Is it convenient to take a look it? '

'Yes, she had. '

As soon as Xiao meng finishes speaking,

She runs to Jiang Yihui's former room quickly.

After a few minutes,

Xiao meng returns to the living room.

Has a booklet in her hand.

She shows it to Yang Ru.

The booklet is extremely elaborate!

Brown pure leather cover— there is also a leather ring button on it.

The ring button can completely seal the written content inside.

Jiang Yihui also made the four words with yellow cloth on the cover:

'Yihui's recipes set'

Yang Ru opened the leather ring button,

Flips through the booklet page by page.

Focuses on every words.

It is actually a wonderful writing recipes set!

It contains:

Foreign desserts:

Orange flavored soufflé, matcha pudding, coconut jelly...

Various snacks:

Taro rice noodle, duck shred wonton, fried crab dumpling...

Some home——made side dishes.

Yang Ru looks at 'Yihui's recipes set' from beginning to end.

Then, reads it again from end to beginning.

But can't find the method of making osmanthus cake .

He even tries to look for traces of osmanthus cake from these recipes.

Still gets nothing!

The ticking rain comes from out door.

A thin layer of mist condenses on the window.

It is full of depression and chill of early winter in Taipei.

In Yang Ru's attic,

It just shows warmth!

Blue mountain coffee is bursting into heat from the cups on the table.

Fruit muffins give off attractive color and aroma.

The sad and shout tune of the English song 'Torn between tow
lovers' is non—stop spinning around the house.
Xiao meng sits peacefully and sweetly beside Yang Ru.
Yang Ru sits quietly.
Sets aside the 'Yihui's recipes set'.
He is silent and thoughtful.
The pursuit for 'red jade talisman' has been stopped for a while.
The osmanthus cake recipe may be one of the two treasures Jiang
Yihui mentioned in stead of trophy.
With Xiao meng's assistance,
Yang Ru searched for the house where Jiang Yihui had lived.
But still didn't find this recipe.
It seems he is ashamed of his great grand father—Yang Jingsong.
He hopes him can give him the power and inspiration to find thing
in heaven!
Unconsciously,
Yang Ru's hands become fists!

'Elder brother Ru...'
'Being with me is a burden to you, right? '
Xiao meng saw that Yang Ru always loved focusing on other
aspects, did not care much about her, could not help asking.
'Nothing happened...'
'You don't think about that. '

'I have some thing in my heart, you know. '

Yang Ru calmed her with words, but still absent—minded.

'You don't need to explain it, I know. '

Xiao meng took a sip of coffee, said frankly.

'You have forgotten all our childhood. '

'Not even a little bit of it is in your memory. '

'And I?'

Xiao men picked the fruit on the muffin with a fork, asked herself.

'Like a camera…'

'Took a complete picture of our past, '

'And put it in my memory. '

'It's just like one lyrics in this song "Torn between two lovers", '

'"Feeling like a fool. ". '

She smiled lightly.

'But it can't be changed, '

'Since I was separated from you, '

'The main memory is the time I spent with you. '

'All other memories are just a foil. '

'It always stays the most prominent place in my memory box! '

Under such a excited confession,

Xiao meng's hand holding the coffee cup's handle shook slightly.

"The main memory is the time I spent with you. "

"All other memories are just a foil. "

"It always stay the most prominent place in my memory box! "

These words of Xiao meng inspires Yang Ru like a brain storm!

Can they be changed like that?

'The other recipes are just for background...'

'The osmanthus cake recipe is the most important! '

'And it is hidden in the most prominent part of the booklet. '

Yang Ru picks up the booklet 'Yihui's recipes set' again.

The most prominent part of it is the brown cover.

Now, he does more research on it.

Realizes that it is a combination of two layers of leather!

'I want to cut its cover...'

Yang Ru held the booklet and looked at Xiao meng like a inquiry.

'It is all up to you, elder brother Ru. '

So Yang Ru cuts the seam between leather with a fruit knife.

'Your aunt Yihui really hid thing!'

Yang Ru shouted in surprised at Xiao meng.

It turns out that many words were engraved on the bottom leather.

Osmanthus cake recipe!

'Since we united, '

'You have been always a key person in my search for items! '

Yang Ru held Xiao men's hands gratefully.

Xiao men just takes his hands away, eyes are full of emotions and says:

'I can be your key person in your life, '

'I should be satisfied too. '

With Xiao meng's consent...

Yang Ru and Gu chang zch takes the address she gave with

osmanthus cake recipe, goes to the countryside to visit solitary

the fourth grandaunt.

The fourth grandaunt's home is in a remote area of the south.

They take a lot of effort to find it.

Her home is still old fashioned courtyard house——siheyuan.

There is a grain——sunning ground of the middle.

The fourth grandaunt receives them in it.

Three persons are just sitting on the bench,

Drink barley tea, peel peanuts and chat casually.

It is a nice trip to the countryside for two urban young people.

When they take out the cover with the osmanthus cake recipe,

The fourth grandaunt was moved to tears!

'You are so kind. '

'Came the all way...'

'Gave me the great gift!'

'He Yi left me, '

'Getting the osmanthus cake recipe is no longer for its content, '

'But through the medium, '

'I can feel the existence of her soul. '

She kept touching the cover and said.

'The young people of today won't consider old man's mind any more. '

'You are exception. '

The fourth grandaunt praised them again.

'Frankly...'

'We have some questions for you. '

Gu chang zch felt a little embarrassed, thought the fourth grandaunt praised them too much.

'Had you seen Jiang Yihui make osmanthus cake? '

He asked the fourth grandaunt.

'Yes, once...'

The fourth grandaunt titled her head, eyebrows and eyes twisted, had some difficulty to remember it.

'I accidentally saw! '

'I had the key of her home, '

'So I could go directly to the house to find her. '

'That time, '

'She happened to be making osmanthus cake in the kitchen. '

'And I knew a little bit about her osmanthus cake making situation. '

'Something special?'

'Such as the appliance or technique she used. '

Gu chang zch hurriedly asked.

'Nohing special.'

'If you have said something…'

'The kitchen was kept clean and fresh while she was making the osmanthus cake. '

'Unlike most people, '

'Make flour, milk every where, '

'Mess up the environment. '

'Anything else?'

Gu chang zch leaned his body slightly to the fourth grandaunt, the attitude seemed a little urgent.

'Think again…'

The fourth grandaunt took a sip of barley tea and slowly began to tell.

'There was such a thing, '

'He Yi pulled out the dry osmanthus from a special container. '

'The container had not been seen in Taiwan. '

'Its shape is Fuji Mountain, transparent glass material. '

She used her hands to create a mountain shape to strengthen the image.

'Clear blue mountain, '

'The mountain top covers snow——this part is a lid that can be opened. '

'When He Yi saw me notice the container, she explained:

'"It is a souvenir from a very important person in my life. "

"I am used to putting the dry osmanthus in it. "

"Their fragrance will be double. "

"The steamed osmanthus cake is also particularly refreshing and smooth. ". '

'How could this happen? '

The Fourth grandaunt covered her mouth and laughed.

'That should be her psychological effect! '

'And I don't want to spoil her fun and echoed her. '

She said intimately.

Gu chang zch just jumps from bench, put his hands on her shoulders, exclaims excitedly:

'The Fourth grandaunt...'

'The information you provided is too great! '

Left the fourth grandaunt's place,

Gu chang zch and Yang Ru walk to the station.

When they set feet to a country path,

Gu chang zch hurries to Yang Ru:

'Did you hear that? '

' The fourth grandaunt mentioned, '

'Jiang Yihui had a container for dry osmanthus. '

'It' s Fuji Mountain type. '

'And it' s a very important person to give her. '

'That person should be Mr. Yamada. '

Gu chang zch slowed down, thought.

'Would that be the case? '

'Before Jiang Yihui died, '

'She took out the dry osmanthus of the container, '

'Put the" red jade talisman" into it. '

'Stored the most precious item in the container sent by lover.'

'This was also very natural manifestation of human nature, right? '

Gu chang zch pulled Yang Ru like he was anxious to get his

approval.

Yang Ru dosen't answer, only considers for while, and takes a few

steps forwards.

And then he turns around and responds:

'A shot in the dark...'

'Tell Xiao meng to look around the house, '

'See if we can make this" mountain" appear. '

He was calm, showed no expression.

Gu chang zch undestands:

Yang Ru no longer expected too much of any clues to find ' red

jade talisman',

Saved himself from suffering disappointment again.

Xiao meng doesn't take the container out of the kitchen cabinet.

But from the dresser in Jiang Yihui's bed room.

'It seemed that Jiang Yihui didn't only take it as a container. '

'And used it for decoration.'

'Beautifully placed!'

Gu chang zch opened the snow cover on the' Fuji Mountain',
smiled and talked.

There is a taste of sweet osmanthus floating from the' Mountain'!
But Gu chang zch finds a red oval object from it instead of dry
osmanthus!

He hands it over to Yang Ru, says:

'You help me to identify it. '

'Is it a real" red jade talisman"? '

Yang Ru holds it in his palm.

The words that his great grand father—Yang Jingsong left his
younger generations appear in front of him.

'"Red jade talisman"— the symbol of supreme power in Tao world,
likes an egg, smooth and flawless, take a close look at it, can see its
internal light shadow and water wave flow, there is a red jade with
the above characteristics, it is a real thing! '

Unconsciously...

Yang Ru's eyes are attracted by the changing light shadow and
water wave in the ' red jade talisman'.

As if they carries the drift and vicissitudes of the ' red jade
talisman' in Tao world!

End

The brilliance of crystal and jade

When Wu Maolin takes the' red jade talisman' from Gu chang zch,

he weeps with joy.

'Ah, it's real" red jade talisman"! '

'My father used it to help patients. '

He held the' red jade talisman' up and watched.

'I spent most of my life...'

'Can't find this treasure.'

'And you guys found it in less than a year. '

'Still juniors are capable! '

He put a thumb on Gu chang zch, Yang Ru.

'It's all Yang Ru's contribution. '

'I was just his assistant. '

Gu chang zch said modestly.

'But every decisive moment was up to you! '

Yang Ru didn't want to claim credit for himself and became

arrogant.

'Oh, well...'

'You don't be humble anymore. '

'You all have credit! '

Wu Maolin put down the' red jade talisman' and put his hands on
the backs of each of them.
Like a fair judge.

'The next question is...'
'Who should keep the" red jade talisman"? '
Wu Maolin was troubled to say.
'I am old and not suitable for this responsibility. '
He stroked his temple.
'Both of you are of good characters, '
'Can also be the owners of" red jade talisman"! '
He turned his aim to Gu chang zch and Yang Ru.
'Oh, no, no...'
Gu chang zch hurriedly waved away to refuse.
'My inner desires are still strong. '
'I am not sure I will do thing right. '
Yang Ru also quickly refuses:
'I am not the right person either. '
'I always fly from one place to another. '
'It is unsafe that " red jade talisman" follows me. '
Wu Maolin sees that two young men have no intention of
inheriting the treasure,
No longer forces them.
'In this case...'

'I have to find someone else. '

Wu Maolin closed his eyes, thinking hard.

After a few minutes,

He opens his eyes and says:

'One person was born in Taoism family. '

'But his ancestors did not follow the established pattern of learning Taoism. '

'Created another fraction to practice.'

'Lived the caves.'

'Drunk dews, ate wild fruits. '

'Even took poison insects and stone power as staple food. '

'Leaped over cliffs.'

'Swimmed in the rapids.'

'Held fire balls and stepped on fire. '

'To get strong body and to build ability to resistant fire and floods!'

'When they practiced this Taoism, '

'Should shut themselves, '

'Didn't interact with people.'

'Wow! '

Gu chang zch couldn't help crying.

'These people were simply supermen! '

'Yet they could stand one twig without falling to the ground. '

'Feet landed without sound. '

'Even they reached the highest level of shadowlessness in Taoism !'

Wu Maolin sincerely praised.

'I just knew the faction in Taoism because of looking for" red jade talisman", '

'All kinds of unique skills of it…'

'Tao like and non —Tao like!'

'Or they can be called specialization, Taoism in Taoism! '

'It is called"Cave bright "faction. '

'But you want to acquire these skills of"Cave bright "faction…'

'It's too hard! '

'And from time to time, '

'They can be threats to life. '

'So…'

Wu Maolin's voice slowed down.

'Few of their offspring inherit these stunts. '

'And this one I say…'

'Just learned some.'

'So this person is still connected with Tao. '

'He is isolated from the world, living alone in the mountain. '

'He is a strange man, called Net Taoist. '

'He is not in the world, but knows the world. '

'My great grand father was also this type of person. '

Yang Ru didn't forget to praise Yang Jingsong in time.

'I give him the " red jade talisman"… '

'It's not unnecessary for him to keep it…'

'But he maybe able to find the best hiding place to this thing. '

Wu Maolin said.

156

Wu Maolin, Yang Ru and Gu chang zch come to Net Taoist's
residence in mountain.

This residence is just a humble hut.

Look it from outside...

The equipment in the house is not comprehensive.

From the point of view of modern people,

It's really difficulty to adapt to a such living environment.

But Net Taoist himself is clear and harmonious.

Smooth skin, dark and beautiful hair color.

Looks like a young man!

　'Net Taoist is descendant of"Cave bright "faction, has been living

　clean life, no desires in heart, years left no trace on him. '

All three of them thought so.

After Wu Maolin introduced Yang Ru, Gu chang zch to Net Taoist,

He just invites them into the hut.

Several people sit on chairs converted from wooden boxes.

Drink mountain spring water.

The water is in homemade pottery cups.

'Brother Maolin...'

Net Taoist made a bow with hands folded in front of Wu Maolin.

'It's been more than 20 years since we last met.'

'At that time, '

'You were quite worried about your father's death and " red jade talisman"stolen. '

'Had always wanted to find the killer and lost article. '

'Today...'

'You come to see me again. '

'Presumably...'

'You have got some thing on your mind. '

He knew it in heart.

'Thanks for these two brave male lions. '

Wu Maolin looked at Yang Ru and Gu chang zch sitting on his left and right sides separately.

'They were regardless of their danger. '

'Made steady efforts.'

'Just helped me find" red jade talisman" out. '

'Most likely one of 'Seven elites in Tao faction'—Yan changrong killed my father and stole it. '

'But not 100% sure.'

'The only sure thing is...'

'His offspring—Yan Chenzhao, the owner of"Hui Qui"shop, once held" red jade talisman". '

'Alas...'

'But no matter whom killer was...'

'After such a long time, '

'He should pass away. '

'This hatred has to end. '

Wu Maolin regretted but said a little relief.

'Hatred hovering in your heart is a big burden. '

'Let it go! '

'You feel free from anxiety. '

Net Taoist agreed with him.

'The" red jade talisman" was with Yan Chenzhao and was late moved elsewhere. '

'Listened to these two young people, '

Wu Maolin paused and watched Yang Ru and Gu chang zch again.

'It belonged to one of "Seven elites in Tao faction"——He Lei's descendant. '

'This person is a woman. '

'But she left world early. '

'They just have ability. '

'Although after many setbacks, '

'In the end...'

He is a bit tired, so drinks some water, rests and go on.

'It was through the woman's adopted daughter called Xiao meng to get back" red jade talisman"! '

The lines of his face were all relaxed.

Gu chang zch, Yang Ru exchang a regret look.

Both feel:

Wu Maolin described the process of finding thing too simply!

The thrilling murder and intense love were all deleted.

Made their journey sounds bland and climax less.

'I know you...'

'You may not want dominate this supreme treasure of Tao world. '

'But you can give it the strongest protection and appropriate placement. '

Wu Maolin solemnly took out the ' red jade talisman' and gave it to Net Taoist.

Net Taoist is holding this treasure but hesitates a little.

'There is a secret...'

'It's the time to mention it. '

Net Taoist seemed to have made the great determination.

'The founder of"Cave bright "faction was Xingtionzi. '

'He was rejected by many orthodox Taoists. '

'But Pangu Zhenren, the leader of Tao world at that time. '

'Just appreciated him very much.'

'He thought Xingtionzi opened up a new realm of Taoism! '

'His heart of Taoism was more pure. '

'Pangu Zhenren entrusted Xingtionz with an" amethyst wall "before he died. '

'And tell him...'

'It was the true authority of the Tao world! '

'It gathered the spirit of heaven, earth and past ancestors. '

'Although" red jade talisman" was powerful, '

'It was not as good as "amethyst wall ". '

'But people circulated erroneous reports. '

'The" red jade talisman" had become a treasure that most of people competed for in Tao world. '

'Pangu Zhenren thought it might be a good thing. '

'This was tantamount to cover "amethyst wall ". '

'That's it...'

'" Amethyst wall "was passed down from generation to generation in our"Cave bright "faction privately. '

'Pangu Zhenren did not pass to" amethyst wall "to his next successor as usual. '

'And gave it to Xingtionzi.'

'I can understand. '

Wu Maolin blinked his eyes and said.

'Although Xingtionzi started another fraction of Taoism, '

'His accomplishments and virtues far exceeded those of ordinary authority of Taoism. '

'In addition...'

'His reclusive life ensured that" amethyst wall "could not fall into the wrong place. '

He remembered his father how got 'red jade talisman' resonated with Pangu Zhenren's action.

'" Amethyst wall "was passed on by"Cave bright "faction. '

'Now...'

'It is in the hands of my generation. '

As soon as Net Taoist finishing speaking,

End   The brilliance of crystal and jade

He goes inside to take thing.

Only a while,

Three of them see an amethyst object stand between Net Taoist's palms!

About a foot long, likes a small cliff.

Even if they have seen all kinds crystals,

But never encounter such a shining one!

After a few minutes of studing this strange thing,

The three just hurriedly look away...

Because this old man and these two young people feel at the same time:

There seemed to be an invisible suction coming out of ' amethyst wall'.

Like sucking their soul!

Net Taoist had expected this result, so he explains so:

'A while ago, '

'I mentioned...'

'" Amethyst wall " gathered the spirit of heaven, earth and past ancestors. '

'If it is manipulated by the wicked, '

'can make people be unconscious or die! '

'You all felt its destructive power. '

'But you don't have to be scared. '

He reverted to his original ease.

'Purely manipulate it, '

'It can cure illness, build health and cultivate mind. '

Net Taoist was quite religious, simply worshiped as ' amethyst wall'
a god.

'" Red jade talisman" also has same effect. '

Yang Ru protested unconvinced.

'Oh, this is of course. '

Net Taoist echoed, then, he smiles subtlety and says:

'But" amethyst wall "'s energy is much higher than" red jade
talisman"'s! '

'Ok...'

'I fully understand. '

Gu chang zch hated to say.

'" Red jade talisman" is just a smoked bomb. '

'The more people fight hard for it, the more secure" amethyst
wall " will be. '

'This kind of Taoism is really horrible, horrible! '

At this moment...

Gu chang zch is like a defeated cock, sitting paralyzed on a chair.

'You don't have to be too disappointed. '

'And don't be angry. '

Net Taoist gently exhorted.

'" Red jade talisman" is also a treasure of Tao world! '

'If" red jade talisman" and " amethyst wall "can be used together in the true energy we practice, '

'That will surely carry forward the purpose of exorcism and controlling desires in Taoism. '

'The chance of bring two items together is very small and very difficulty. '

Net Taoist's attitude was both sentimental and excited.

'May be this thing is not known to everyone. '

'But the three of you did make an uncommon contribution in the Tao world. '

He puts ' amethyst wall' down.

After thanking the three of them...

Net Taoist juxtaposes 'amethyst wall' with ' red jade talisman' in front of them.

Instantly...

Purple and red set off each other!

Crystal bright and jade light add radiance and beauty each other!

Make a rare dazzling picture!

Wu Maolin, Yang Ru and Gu chang zch walk out of Net Taoist's hut and don't immediately go down the mountain.

Every one has been unwilling to talk or move for a while .

They only faced a large mountain, standing and thinking.

'I feel like breaking love again. '

'My whole heart is hollowed out. '

Gu chang zch couldn't help but be the first to speak.

'I thought we had succeeded in carrying out uncle lin's assign. '

'Found the priceless treasure of Taoism! '

'Don't expect it to be the second product. '

His tone was dispirited.

'I consider myself to be a talented person. '

Yang Ru folded his arms on his chest and said confidently.

'My family had been entangled for generations. '

'But they were unable to detect the whereabouts of " red jade talisman". '

'And in my generation, '

'I would find the answer. '

'Sure enough!'

'Something was found. '

'But it is not the original mean at all .'

'God just played a big joke for me! '

The descendant of 'Seven elites in Tao faction' looked extremely angry, the overlapping hands turned into fists.

'Don't say that...'

'"I am old and take it easy. ". '

Gu chang zch saw what Wu Maolin wanted to say something to them, so he took the lead in blocking and said.

'No, you totally misunderstood me. '

'I am not trying to flaunt my old age in front of you. '

Wu Maolin hastily denied.

'I know it. '

'It' s difficulty for everyone to accept this result. '

'Might as well look at it from another respect.'

'All the time, '

'We just focused on finding" red jade talisman". '

'And didn't notice the enlightenment and value brought to
everyone's living in the process. '

Yang Ru and Gu chang zch heared what Wu Maolin said, can' t help
but hang their heads sideways, think about something tentatively.

'Do not deny...'

Gu chang zch talked slowly.

'The" red jade talisman" was equivalent to saving my life. '

'In addition, '

'There was a chance to catch the" Gold Star"train! '

'In such an amazingly luxurious and narrow train cabin...'

'Met so many weird characters!'

'It's almost in heterodimensional space. '

'Well, '

'This train trip gave me a new horizon! '

His original anger face suddenly relaxed.

'I had never met someone like this...'

Gu chang zch turned towards Yang Ru.

'It's so amazing to be able to change gender. '

'And it worked! '

Listened to Gu chang zch, Yang Ru's complexion gradually ease.

'I come from Taoist family. '

'Always practice Taoism as the root of the life. '

'But in order to find this so called "supreme treasure in Tao world "

blindly identified by people. '

'Just contacted with ninjas world of Japan!'

'Met Mr. Yamada, '

'And carefully explored the inner nature of a ninja.'

'Saw a person that could live so freely and persistently! '

'I really lost to him. '

Speaking of Yamada, Yang Ru was in a state of excitement again.

Wu Maolin seems to have seen them through.

'You two young people all injected new ideas for life because you

looked for" red jade talisman". '

'The process widened each other's field of vision. '

'And you have become more energetic and stronger. '

He observed and judged them one more time.

'As for me...'

Wu Maolin smiled openly.

'If I gave up looking for "red jade talisman" and murder early.'

'Then I might have a secure and peaceful life. '

'But it's also tasteless and insipid. '

'I had been hurt and deceived for this thing. '

'And even suffered many blood disasters!'

'But under these storms, '

'My temper became tuned. '

'I am able to be hard and soft. '

'Can flex and stretch. '

'I often think, '

'When I am going to die…'

'My brain will flash some fragments of my past life. '

'I will definitely realize the richness of the part of finding " red jade talisman". '

'And will confess to not wasting life! '

There was an admirable detachment on his wrinkled old face.

'Yeah!'

Gu chang zch turned back by accident, but called out unexpectedly.

With his scream…

Wu Maolin, Yang Ru naturally turns around.

So they met,

There two lights coming out of Net Taoist's hut!

One is the clear purple light like a flowing water band.

The other is a more intense and colorful light.

They cross and shine.

It's like a purple stream with a bright ribbon.

The scene looks really shocking!

'It seems to run into Aurora! '

Gu chang zch was quite excited to describe.

'No, It's more precious! '

'Aurora had appeared too many times. '

'It's first time that " red jade talisman" and " amethyst wall " two treasures had met! '

'Under each other's spiritual agitation...'

'The" red jade talisman" broke through the limit that shone once in ten years. '

'Shines with" amethyst wall ". '

'It is a miracle! '

Wu Maolin looked at the wonder of two brilliance, exultantly explained.

'Answer revealed! '

Yang Ru said slowly.

'It turned out that we were not looking for the single" red jade talisman". '

'But the brilliance that" red jade talisman" interweaved with" amethyst wall ". '

'It is also a symbol of the ultimate spirit of true Taoism !'

Two light continue to strengthen.

They seem to hear the conversation between the old man and two

End   The brilliance of crystal and jade

young people.

Then, jump together, put on three people's heads.

Wu Maolin, Yang Ru and Gu chang zch are shrouded in these two kinds of exotic light...

The whole person seems to have bee washed.

Body and mind are full of positive energy!

A joy of sublimation is leaking from their hearts little by little.

And this is what they didn't feel when they got ' red jade talisman'.

THE END

Finished it at 12: 50 on January20 2017

Corrected it at 21: 45 on May27 2017